MEN
in
UNIFORM

**Courteous, courageous and commanding—
these heroes lay it all on the line for the
people they love in more than fifty stories about
loyalty, bravery and romance.
Don't miss a single one!**

DEBRA WEBB

SPECIAL ASSIGNMENT: BABY

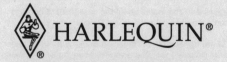

TORONTO • NEW YORK • LONDON
AMSTERDAM • PARIS • SYDNEY • HAMBURG
STOCKHOLM • ATHENS • TOKYO • MILAN • MADRID
PRAGUE • WARSAW • BUDAPEST • AUCKLAND

Recycling programs
for this product may
not exist in your area.

ISBN-13: 978-0-373-36266-0

SPECIAL ASSIGNMENT: BABY

Copyright © 2001 by Harlequin Books S.A.

Debra Webb is acknowledged as the author of Special Assignment: Baby.

www.eHarlequin.com

Printed in U.S.A.

DEBRA WEBB

wrote her first story at age nine and her first romance at thirteen. It wasn't until she spent three years working for the military behind the Iron Curtain and within the confining political walls of Berlin, Germany, that she realized her true calling. A five-year stint with NASA on the space shuttle program reinforced her love of the endless possibilities within her grasp as a storyteller. A collision course between suspense and romance was set. Debra has been writing romantic suspense and action-packed romantic thrillers since. Visit her at www.DebraWebb.com or write to her at P.O. Box 4889, Huntsville, AL 35815.

Writing has always been my dream
for as long as I can remember. The opportunity
to express myself in this art form and to touch my
readers means more to me than words can convey.
Life is far too short sometimes, and because of that
injustice there are those who never fully reach the dream
that lived so vibrantly in their hearts and souls.
But we must believe that God holds a special place
for them where their every dream will come true.
This book is dedicated to a fine lady who dreamed of
writing the stories that lived in her heart—
Bobbie Waite, beloved mother and aspiring author.
Though she is sorely missed, Bobbie's hopes and dreams
live on forever in the lives she touched.

PROLOGUE

"WE'RE PLEASED TO have you with us, Court." The man smiled, the kind of smile politicians used to get your vote. His voice was deep and disturbingly calm.

Careful to analyze every move, every look, Court Brody grasped the hand Joshua Neely offered and shook it firmly. "I'm honored to be here, sir," he said with as much sincerity as he could marshal.

"My friends call me Joshua," the older man returned with an ease that was both confident and knowing. "And I think you and I are going to be friends." That smile again. "Raymond tells me that you're very interested in our beliefs."

"I am." Court resisted the urge to scrub his palm against his jeans when Neely released it. "I've been away for a long time. But now that I'm back home where I belong, I'd like to be a part of what your people are doing."

Neely nodded his understanding. "Raymond, take Court and show him around. We'll give him his official welcome at the rally tonight."

"Yes, sir, Joshua."

Grinning as if he'd just accomplished a major coup, Raymond ushered Court toward the nearest exit. On the stoop leading out of the enormous meeting hall, he paused and slapped Court on the shoulder.

"I knew he'd invite you to join us right away. I knew it," Raymond repeated, his tall, thin frame fairly vibrating with excitement. "That's why I wanted you to come today. We need more men like you, Court. We've got to fight if we're gonna bring this country back to what it should be."

Court recalled the crowd of men, women and children gathered in the meeting hall for Neely's speech. The hour-long monologue he'd just endured reminded him entirely too much of a Sunday morning fire-and-brimstone sermon. Only it was Saturday, and this place, with its security fence and armed guards, was no church. Yet, Joshua Neely certainly fit the bill of preacher. Court had a niggling feeling that the man was anything but godly. Tall, with just enough gray around the temples to look distinguished, Neely made an impressive picture. No wonder people around here were flocking to him as if he were the answer to the second coming.

"I appreciate you bringing me, Raymond." Court plowed his hand through his hair and settled his black Stetson into place, then shifted uncertainly, playing his part. Good old Raymond had swallowed the act hook, line and sinker the moment he and Court met at the Watering Hole. The guy was desperate to bring in a few new recruits. "I've been back a couple of weeks already and haven't quite figured out what I want to do with myself. I'm sure glad I ran into you yesterday."

That wacky grin split the other man's face again. "Whatever you're looking for, buddy, you'll find it right here." Raymond ushered Court down the steps, anxious to show him around. "Joshua provides us with everything we need, and all he asks in return is loyalty." He fixed Court with a you-know-what-I-mean look. "*Complete* loyalty."

Before Court could utter the response poised on the tip of his tongue, a tall figure, definitely female, rushed around the corner of the building and skidded to a stop directly in front of them. Raymond backed up a step to let the woman, who was clearly in a hell of a hurry, pass. Court surveyed her speculatively, then froze. His heart dropped all the way to his well broken-in boots.

Sabrina.

For a full ten seconds all he could do was look at her. Still tall and thin, with a luscious mixture of caramel-and-honey-colored hair falling around her shoulders, she stared right back at him. Those eyes—Court swallowed tightly—dark chocolate brown, wide with long lashes tipped in gold. Right now those gorgeous eyes were registering the same shock as Court's own no doubt were. God, it felt like a lifetime since he'd seen her.

"Court?"

His name was hardly more than a whisper on her full lips, but the sound was enough to snap him out of the trance he'd drifted into.

"What're you doing here?" A questioning frown pleated her smooth brow.

"Court's my new recruit," Raymond enthused before Court could fully gather his wits. "You know him, Sabrina?"

She knew him, all right. Adrenaline pounded through

Court's veins. Sabrina Korbett was the only person in this godforsaken place that knew he was a special agent for the Federal Bureau of Investigation.

"Yes," she said, confused. "But I thought—"

"It's been a long time," Court interrupted smoothly as he grabbed her by the shoulders and jerked her against him. "Too long." Inclining his head to the right, he closed his mouth over hers before she could fully comprehend his intent. She tensed, but in no time at all she surrendered to his kiss…just like before.

She was soft, and warm, and her mouth opened for his as if two years hadn't passed since they'd laid eyes on each other. As if…the past hadn't happened at all. He accepted her instinctive invitation, his tongue sliding along hers, his fingers automatically tightening around her slender arms. The same need that had always filled him when he so much as looked at Sabrina washed over him now, making him weak with want, making his blood boil in his veins.

"Guess you know each other pretty well. I'll… ah…just wait over by the training center," Raymond announced, breaking the fragile connection that had whisked Court back into the past he'd tried so hard to forget.

Sabrina flattened her palms against his chest and tried to push him away. He knew he had to stop, but, *damn,* he didn't want to. The feel of her touch, even knowing that she was pushing him away, arced through him.

"Stop," she managed to blurt between his stolen kisses.

Court drew back just far enough to look into those wide, startled eyes. He focused his most intimidating glare down at her. "You don't know me anymore, Brin, so don't say anything we'll both regret."

She wrenched out of his grasp and glared back at him. Court knew the instant she'd made her decision. He braced himself for the blow.

Sabrina slapped him hard.

He deserved it.

"I don't know what you're doing back here, Court Brody," she said hotly, her breath still ragged from his kiss. "And I don't care, but I want you to stay away from me."

Court held her gaze for two beats longer, as difficult as that proved with her glaring daggers at him and his lips yearning to mate with hers once more. "Just remember what I said, and we'll both be *safe.*"

She blinked and uncertainty replaced some of the fury in her eyes. "Is…this some sort of undercover job?" Anxiety tightened the pretty features of her face. "You're not…are you here to—"

He forced a bitter laugh. "Hate to disappoint you, but I'm not that guy anymore. *You don't know me.*"

He walked away without looking back. His heart skipped a beat or two as he struggled to calm his breathing. Raymond was waiting, probably wondering what was up with the little episode of "remember when" that Court and Sabrina had just played out. Now he'd have to figure out a way to explain that kiss.

Damn.

Just what he needed—he swore again—to get his cover made before he even got started with this assignment. Court blew out a breath as he strode in the direction of the training center. It never once entered his mind that he might run into her at this militia compound. Sabrina should be married and raising a family by now.

Court clenched his jaw at the thought of her with another man.

She sure as hell didn't belong to him. And Sabrina Korbett was a distraction he didn't need right now. Especially not *here*.

Getting into the compound had been easy.

Now all he had to do was stay alive until he got the information he needed.

But Sabrina knew his secret. If she told anyone what she knew, all the information in the world wouldn't do Court any good.

Because he'd be a dead man.

CHAPTER ONE

Why had he come back here?

Halfway down the mile-long dirt-and-gravel driveway, Court Brody slowed the old truck he had purchased for this assignment to a stop and surveyed the Lonesome Pony ranch. Though not the same ranch he had grown up on, the scene was all too familiar. A wide stream curved through the property like a winding snake. The towering mountain ranges served as a backdrop for a picture straight off the pages of a calendar. A large barn and corral sat in the distance, beyond the trees that bordered the house and yard. Though more modern, the big rambling house with its sprawling front porch reminded him of the one he *hadn't* lived in as a kid growing up in Montana.

Nope. His family had occupied a much smaller place just far enough away from the big house to know he didn't really belong, but not quite far enough away to ignore what he was missing. Court swallowed the bitterness that welled in his throat at the memories.

His family had been dirt poor. Once his pathetic excuse for a father had died, he and his three bothers had scattered apart like so much dust in the wind. But he had landed on his feet. He'd gotten his college degree by working hard and earning a scholarship. Then he'd joined the Bureau. He had what he wanted now—money, prestige and a great condo as far away from this damned place as he could get and still remain in the continental United States. His brothers hadn't done so badly either.

"Enough, Brody," Court grumbled. Coming back here wasn't his idea, but he would make the best of it because it was his job. And Courtland Brody never failed at his job. He was good. He knew it, and the Bureau knew it as well. If Daniel Austin and the rest of his Montana Confidential crew didn't know it yet, they soon would. Whether they ever wanted to admit it or not. Court knew the business of undercover work.

A division of the Federal Department of Safety, Montana Confidential worked in a way the Bureau couldn't. The agents lived and worked a ranch, thus blending in with the locals. The Bureau, acting as Big Brother, offered to lend a hand in getting the Montana operation off the ground. Translation: Court's new assignment, infiltrate the militia and determine what leader Joshua Neely was up to. Not such a bad assignment had it been any place else on the planet. There were far too many memories here that he didn't want to relive. Too many faces he didn't want to see…couldn't bear to see.

Disgusted with himself for loitering in the past, Court drove the rest of the way to the house and parked behind Daniel Austin's truck. It was Saturday and most of the crew appeared to be on the porch enjoying the late August afternoon. Thankfully it wasn't as hot as it had been the past couple of days. He might as well get this over with. Court emerged from the vehicle and strode toward the house.

Not surprisingly, Dale McMurty was the first to greet him. Dale and her husband, Patrick, were locals and friendly to a fault. Exactly the kind of people he'd left behind eleven years ago. He didn't want anyone close, and the McMurtys liked to get close. The elderly couple served as caretakers for the ranch Montana Confidential used as a home base. Just one more reason he was glad to be bunking at the compound now.

"Howdy, Court," Dale shouted, hands propped on her apron-clad, ample hips. She appraised him from head to toe as he stepped up onto the porch. "Now, that's more like it, son. You look like you belong on a ranch instead of in some big fancy office."

Court couldn't prevent the half smile that tilted one side of his mouth. Leave it to Dale to praise his thrift-store finds. He needed to fit in, therefore faded jeans and worn shirts were a must. But the boots and hat were his own. Some things a man couldn't compromise on. No matter how long he lived in the city, he didn't think he would ever find anything that wore better than a good pair of boots.

"You look like the Marlboro man," Whitney MacNair, Austin's executive assistant, noted, approval in her crisp voice. As usual, she looked like a model off the cover of *Cosmopolitan* magazine.

"Thank you, ladies," Court acknowledged with a tip of his hat. Dale was likely just being nice, Court knew, but Whitney—the fashion queen—was another story. "I couldn't exactly waltz into Neely's compound wearing Armani, now could I?"

Whitney pretended to consider that option for a moment, then grinned. "Guess not, cowboy."

Court resisted the wicked urge to ask her if she knew the UPS man on a first-name basis yet. The wilds of Montana might not offer a Gucci store for the diehard in-vogue shopper, but Whitney had discovered a direct connection to her favorite big-city shops on the Internet. And UPS was more than happy to deliver.

Frank Connolly, one of the agents assigned to Confidential, nodded a hello in Court's direction, but he was too busy attending to his new wife to pay Court any real mind. And C.J. definitely had eyes only for Frank. She shot Court a quick smile just the same. He had to admit that the two made a nice couple. A wistful feeling welled inside of him, but he brutally squashed it. He didn't need a relationship like that…he had the Bureau.

Jewel, the McMurtys' usually vivacious twelve-year-old granddaughter, looked about as solemn-faced as a lonesome filly separated from the rest of the herd. Court wondered if Frank and C.J.'s wedding was the reason for her sad expression. The kid had herself a king-size crush on the ex-military pilot. Frank's sudden marriage to C.J. obviously didn't sit well with the kid. Well, Court could certainly sympathize with that.

Marriage was just like family—overrated.

More greetings were exchanged before Court made his way to the man he needed to see. Daniel Austin, head of operations, stood at the far end of the porch looking out over the ranch. The place was shaping up rather well, Court had to admit. And Austin was the driving force behind the evolution. A former dude ranch, the Lonesome Pony had every amenity one could wish for in the wilds of horse country, including a fancy pool and private cabins. Austin had done a good job pulling this setup together in a short period of time.

Court wondered, though, as he came up next to Austin, if this would ever be enough for the man. Court had the distinct impression that something was missing. Maybe Austin was another victim of the wedding bell blues. The man was obviously still in love with his ex-wife, and missed his son immensely.

Just another reason, Court mused, to steer clear of the troubling entanglement of marriage. He didn't want to know the kind of regrets and pain being separated from a child could bring.

Austin met Court's gaze then, and studied him a moment before he spoke. "What went wrong?"

Before Court even opened his mouth, the man knew. He was smart, and too wise for Court's comfort. Of course, it didn't take a rocket scientist to know that Court wouldn't have bothered stopping by so early in the operation unless he felt it absolutely necessary. "I ran into an old friend," he admitted quietly.

"I thought you didn't have any connections here."

Court heard the concern in the older man's voice. Both knew just how risky this business could be. There was no room for guesswork.

"Just one." One he had banished from his mind two years ago, Court didn't add. One he should have forgotten, but hadn't really—at least not on the level he needed to. And he'd definitely tried.

"Give me his name and I'll have Kyle or Frank take care of it."

"*Her* name is Sabrina Korbett." Court let go a weary breath. "And I can take care of her myself. She won't give me up."

Surprise evident in his expression, Austin asked, "You're sure about that?"

Court nodded. "She's the only one who knows. She wouldn't purposely put me in danger, but…" He took a moment to consider his words. "But she might not understand, so I'll have to talk to her." He shrugged. "Make up some kind of acceptable excuse."

Austin rubbed his chin thoughtfully. "She's that kind of connection, huh?"

"She used to be." Court pretended to survey the landscape he'd just as soon not lay eyes on again. Austin was studying him, attempting to read his thoughts. Measuring the risk.

"I've met Sabrina, even bought some mares from her," Austin told him. "She seems nice enough." He leveled his too-knowing gaze on Court's. "But watch your step," he advised sagely. "A woman can be your best friend, or your worst enemy. Even one as sweet as Sabrina."

Court suffered his own little jolt of surprise at the knowledge that Austin knew Sabrina. Just another possibility he hadn't considered. It seemed his old life was determined to get all twisted up with his new one. And he didn't want that to happen.

"I just came by to let you know that I'm in," Court said abruptly, effectively changing the subject. "They're going to make it official at the rally tonight."

"Let's take a walk," Austin suggested.

Court followed Austin across the porch and to the steps. Before he could get away completely, C.J.'s English-accented voice stopped him. "Whitney and Kyle are laying odds on who will walk down the aisle next. What's your opinion, Agent Brody?" she asked.

Deliberately, Court turned back to face both the question and the lady. Her cheeks darkened as if she'd only just realized how forward her question sounded. "I wouldn't dream of speculating, *Mrs. Connolly,* but I can guarantee you it won't be me."

A knowing smile tilted the lovely scientist's mouth. "Never say never, *Agent Brody,*" she warned.

"When my daddy gets married, I'm gonna be the f'ower girl," Molly, Kyle Foster's daughter, announced in her most enthusiastic three-year-old voice, from her position in her daddy's lap. Kyle only shook his head in dismay.

Court gifted the little girl with a smile and quickly turned away from the other speculative gazes. He didn't care what they laid odds on as long as they left him out of it. Kyle, the second agent assigned to support Montana Confidential, should have learned his lesson as well. Court had heard the rumors about how the guy's ex-wife had dumped him and the kid. Court shook his head as he followed Austin away from the house. Walking away from a defunct marriage was one thing, but leaving a kid was unspeakable.

Just another reason that "never" was exactly when Court planned to marry. The image of Sabrina suddenly loomed large in his mind, but he pushed it away. Whatever they had once shared, it was long gone now. There was nothing between them anymore but his guilt, her hurt and a lingering spark of leftover physical attraction.

"The vet stopped by yesterday," Austin said, drawing Court's wayward attention back to him. "That prize-winning mare we were lucky enough to purchase was successfully bred with the new stallion."

Court glanced at the pasture beyond the corral where the stallion grazed. The animal was a beauty. A dark bay with a white blanket and spots. Court propped one arm on the top rail of the corral and surveyed the other mares scattered about beyond the stallion. Mostly quarter horses and Appaloosas, he noted, remembering that the Double K, Sabrina's ranch, had specialized in Appys. The thought was accompanied by another image of Sabrina and those long, tanned legs. His mouth went dust dry.

Blinking away the image, he snagged his gaze on the one horse that didn't seem to fit with the rest of the herd. An old gelding—Silver, if he remembered right. A mottled white horse, the color of stonework. The bony old fella wasn't good for much other than keeping the McMurtys' granddaughter happy. The girl did love that old horse.

Court snapped his thoughts back to the assignment. Horses weren't his business anymore. Neither were ranches. Hell, he didn't even like being here.

"Is there something else you wanted to say, Austin?" Court knew the man hadn't dragged him away from the others to brag about his breeding expertise. Court already knew more than he wanted to about what people did for a living in Montana. He could teach Austin a thing or two. Including how that fancy helicopter Austin had insisted the Confidential crew needed for rapid deployment could be used for herding horses.

Austin fixed his steady brown gaze on Court's. "I know you think you're not one of us, Court, but you are." He held up his hand when Court would have protested the "teamwork" talk again. "Right now you're assigned to Confidential, and I expect you to remember that."

"I don't think there's much chance I could forget it," Court returned curtly.

"You're a good man, Court, a top-notch agent, but don't think that will keep me from jerking your butt off this assignment if you ignore my orders."

Court gritted his teeth against the instant response that wanted to form on his lips. He knew his job…and he knew the chain of command. Austin didn't need to remind him of either.

"Don't even think about leaving me out of the loop. We're a team. Frank and Kyle are part of that team as well."

"You'll know everything I know," Court assured him patiently. "I'll keep you fully informed."

"Good." Austin's gaze returned to the stallion. "Since I know you're a man of your word, I won't worry about that anymore."

"I'll check in with you as soon as I have anything to pass along."

Court turned and strode toward his truck. He would keep Austin informed…that was his job. But if Austin thought Court was going to follow anybody else's time clock, he had another thought coming.

"Court."

Reluctantly, Court stopped and turned back to the man in charge. "Yeah?"

"Don't forget what I said about women. You can't ever be sure."

Court nodded thoughtfully, then continued toward his destination. Hell, he supposed his next stop should be the Double K. He had to set Sabrina straight right from the start. And he had every intention of finding out what she'd been doing at the militia compound.

Maybe that way she wouldn't haunt his dreams again tonight. Hell, if he'd known that last night's dream of seeing her again was going to be prophetic he'd have avoided today's confrontation. But he hadn't known, and today's little tête-à-tête had proved one thing beyond a shadow of a doubt. He would have to be very, very careful where Sabrina was concerned.

COURT BRAKED TO A STOP in front of the Korbett house and shoved the gearshift into Park. The paint on the looming two-story house was blistered and peeling. A frown tugged at his mouth. He couldn't remember ever seeing the place in this kind of shape. His father had been handy with a paintbrush and he'd spent a lifetime taking care of the Double K. Court blinked away the memories that immediately surfaced from his childhood here. The old man had been handy with a liquor bottle as well. It dawned on Court then that the house probably hadn't been painted since his father died fourteen years ago. His frown deepened again as his gaze shifted to the barn, then the fenced pastures. The whole place was in pretty sad shape.

Where were the horses? He surveyed the empty pastures again. The place had a definite empty feel to it.

The driver's side door groaned as he pushed it open. Court slid from behind the wheel and pushed the door shut amid the sound of another rusty grumble. Sabrina's father had died about five years back, if memory served him right. But Sabrina had seemed fine when Court returned a couple of years ago for his mother's funeral. But then she hadn't done much talking about the ranch or her family. And that was the extent of what he knew regarding the Korbetts these days. Discounting the unexpected way his body still longed for hers.

But that wasn't going to happen.

He and Sabrina had been down that road, and Court felt relatively certain she didn't want to go that route again any more than he did. *I want you to stay away from me.* Her warning had been pretty clear, he decided when the memory pricked his ego.

The house where he'd lived the first nineteen years of his life abruptly caught his eye. As if marching the last mile to his execution, Court headed in that direction. The place was set against the foot of the mountain and nestled in the trees. The Korbetts had called it the springhouse, since a wide spring ran between it and the main house and barn. This time of year the flow of water wouldn't be much more than a trickle. But he remembered vividly the rocks that lay beneath the water. Collecting them had been one of his favorite hobbies as a kid.

Amazingly, the old log-and-chink house had withstood the elements and time far better, it seemed, than the main house.

Court hesitated halfway to the barn. He supposed he should knock on Sabrina's door and let her know he was here. Judging by yesterday's reception, he was likely trespassing at the moment as far as she would be concerned. She wouldn't welcome his presence. Not relishing what he was about to do, Court started toward the porch. He could count on her having questions. Sabrina Korbett had never been the type to let anything go easily—except him. She hadn't once tried to talk him into staying. His sudden appearance now under what could only be called questionable circumstances would pique her natural curiosity.

But somehow he had to make sure she understood where he stood in spite of the fact that he couldn't tell her a single thing.

SABRINA DROPPED the feed buckets near the supply room door and wiped the perspiration from her forehead with her sleeve. She dusted her hands on her faded jeans and sighed with satisfaction. It wasn't much, but it was a start. Both the mares would foal soon. Then she would have four horses rather than two. She wished her father was still alive to give her some badly needed advice. No matter how many years passed, she still missed him…missed the way things used to be when she'd been a skinny kid with nothing to worry about except chasing Court Brody.

Sabrina shook the thought away. She would not think about him right now. She had too much on her plate already.

This spring had been the hardest. With the property

taxes due and no money to live on, she had come dangerously close to losing the ranch, but Daniel Austin had saved her. He had bought her entire herd save for the two mares. He'd even purchased a small portion of her land to go along with the Lonesome Pony since the two properties bordered each other. Though Sabrina hated to start from scratch, and even worse, she hated to part with any of the land, it was the only way to save the ranch. Austin had paid her top dollar, too.

Sabrina smiled. If she were completely honest with herself, she would admit that he paid her more than the goods she sold him were worth. Either the man seemed to sense her desperation or he didn't really know the depressed value of things. Now she had the taxes and insurance paid, and she had enough money in the bank to survive on for a little while. She'd even put back a little something toward college for Charlie. She wouldn't touch that money for anything other than an outright medical emergency. If worse came to worst at this point, she would have to consider a mortgage, and that was assuming she could get approved for a loan. She had nothing left of value to sell.

Except the land, and she wouldn't sell another square foot of the land her father had passed on to her and her brother Charlie.

They would make it.

Somehow.

Sabrina reached up to turn off the baby monitor just as her fifteen-month-old son let out a sleepy sigh. Emotion constricted her throat as her firm resolve not to think about Court crumbled. If he discovered her secret, what would he say? More important, what would he do? He wanted no part of life here. Hadn't for years. Would he be determined to take his son from the only home he had ever known?

Fear slid through her veins. She moistened her lips and forced herself to breathe. She couldn't let that happen. But all it would take was one look. Ryan looked so much like his father. Brown hair streaked with golden highlights. Same gray eyes. Her pulse reacted at the memory of Court's kiss this morning. What in the world was he doing back here? Why would he come back after all this time? Her lips dipped into a frown. Hanging out with men like Raymond Green and Joshua Neely wasn't Court's style. He was smarter than that.

Two years ago when he'd come home for his mother's funeral, Court had been an agent with the FBI. He'd told Sabrina everything about his new life that night, his enthusiasm had been impossible to contain. She swallowed tightly. The night Ryan had been conceived.

His presence at the militia compound just didn't add up. Nor did Charlie's, Sabrina ruminated. Somehow she had to get her brother away from those men. He was only fourteen, too young to understand the evil that men like Neely could do in the name of God and country.

If only her mother hadn't deserted them three years ago. Sabrina shook her head sadly. Like Court, her mother had been only too happy to leave Montana and start a new life. Too bad she left her old one in an uproar, and Sabrina to raise the son she had no time or patience to deal with. It seemed everyone Sabrina loved was destined to leave her one way or the other. But she could count on Ryan. He loved her no matter what.

Heaving a beleaguered sigh, Sabrina snagged the monitor from its shelf, turned it off and strode out of the barn. She couldn't change the past. She thought of Ryan, the only part of the past she didn't want to change. But she could do her best to survive, and to create a good life for her son and her brother.

Sabrina stretched her neck and rolled her shoulders to loosen them up after her barn-cleaning frenzy as she headed back toward the house. She had needed a way to release the pent-up stress related to Court's kiss. The house sparkled after the scrubbing she'd given the place, leaving her no option but to turn her attention to the barn. With Ryan asleep, leaving the house would have been impossible if not for the handy monitor. Thank God for that invention. She couldn't survive without the gadget. She had received it as a shower gift. At first she had been reluctant to use it, but that didn't last long.

Anytime Ryan was asleep, she could do chores and still know that he was sleeping safely in his crib. The monitor was so sensitive she could hear even the slightest change in his breathing. If he woke up, she would know immediately. Her little cleaning venture was just what she had needed to work off some steam this afternoon.

Swiping back a wisp of hair that had escaped her ponytail, Sabrina smoothed a hand down the front of her dusty shirt. Still too flat-chested to worry with a bra, she wondered if Court found her in any way attractive. He'd kissed her. But that was probably nothing more than a spontaneous reaction to seeing her after all this time. She was too tall and too skinny. Court probably had a whole harem of voluptuous blondes back in D.C. She hadn't been woman enough to keep him. Not even after she'd given him her innocence. Her enthusiasm had pushed him away. He'd wanted to get away for as long as she could remember. She shouldn't have been surprised.

Her gaze suddenly lit on an unfamiliar truck parked next to her own. She squinted and tried to make out more details about the beat-up old jalopy. The thing looked worse than hers, and that was saying something. As she neared the house she heard several raps against her front door. Sabrina hastened her step, all but running around the corner of the house. She didn't get many callers these days, and she didn't want this one to inadvertently wake up her sleeping child. She still had more outside work to do.

Who would be dropping by this time of day, anyway? Most folks she knew were busy working until dusk. God, she hoped nothing had happened to Charlie.

A tall, broad-shouldered man, his back turned to her, stood at her front door.

"Can I help you?" she called hesitantly as she neared the porch. There was something familiar about his stance, she decided just as he turned around.

Court.

A chunk of ice formed in Sabrina's stomach. Had someone told him about Ryan? Could he know already? She resisted the impulse to shake her head. That couldn't be. No one knew Court was Ryan's father. No one but the doctor, that is.

"What do you want?" Sabrina asked coldly.

That gray gaze settled onto hers, and Sabrina's heart took an extra foolish beat. How could any man look that good? Mile-wide shoulders, lean waist. She shook herself. This was no time to be admiring Court's many physical assets. He was standing on her porch, only a few feet from where Ryan lay sleeping. She suddenly remembered the monitor she held and quickly tucked it into the back of her waistband. Her heart bumped into high speed.

"We need to talk, Brin."

His voice was low, steady, and too gentle. She didn't want to hear it. She didn't want to look at him. "I'd like you to leave, Court," she said sternly. "You're not welcome here anymore."

Sabrina stood her ground near the steps. She would not give him any remote hope that he might be invited in. To her utter relief he moved across the porch and down the steps, his slow, fluid movements making it difficult for her to breathe. There had always been something about the way he moved. It was more than mere male cockiness…something sensual yet predatory.

"I'm sorry to hear that."

He slowly rotated his hat in his hands, his gaze seemingly uncertain. Could he be nervous? She almost laughed out loud at that notion. The one thing Court Brody had always been was absolutely certain of himself. And with good reason. He was strong, powerfully built, and more intelligent than any man she had ever known.

But his heart was hardened with bitterness and resentment. And nothing Sabrina had ever done had changed that.

"I wish you'd reconsider, Brin."

He still called her *Brin.* No one but Court had ever called her by that nickname past the age of fifteen. Not even her father.

"Don't call me that." She swiped her damp palms against her thighs. "No one calls me that anymore."

"I need you to understand how important being a part of the militia is for me."

His words stunned her. "You are kidding?" she blurted. "You don't see through Neely?" She shook her head in disbelief. "I thought you were some big, hotshot FBI agent. What happened, Court? Did you get bored with that, too?" Lord knew the man had a restless streak a mile wide, one that cut straight through that rock in his chest he called a heart.

He blinked but gave away nothing of his feelings. Just like always, she would never know what he was really feeling.

"I don't want to talk about the Bureau or D.C." He stared at the ground a moment. "I'm trying to put that behind me." His gaze latched onto hers once more. "I want to start over. Here."

If she'd thought he'd stunned her before, she was completely astonished now. "Here?" she parroted. "Now I know you're joking."

A muscle twitched in his chiseled jaw. "Is that so hard to believe?"

Sabrina laughed dryly. "It's downright unfathomable."

Irritation marred his handsome features. "Be that as it may, I'm back. I don't think folks around here would understand about my time in the Bureau. I'd rather you didn't mention it."

"I see," she replied with sudden clarity. "You don't want Brother Neely to know you were once an actual fed, is that it?"

"Don't make this any more difficult than it needs to be, Brin," he warned. This time there was nothing at all gentle about his tone.

He stepped nearer…too close. Sabrina held her ground, despite the butterflies taking flight in her stomach.

"No one else knows but you," he reminded in a low, lethal tone that sent shivers skittering up her spine. "But I'm not worried 'cause I know you wouldn't do anything to make trouble for me."

He had her there. No matter what he'd done in the past. No matter how badly he had hurt her. Sabrina would never do anything to hurt him—except keep her own secret. But that was to protect Ryan, she rationalized, when she knew damn well it was to protect herself. She couldn't lose her son. No way.

She remembered to exhale. "Fine. If that's the way you want it," she said tightly.

Those silvery depths softened then, and he almost smiled. The quirking of his lips was so subtle that had she not been looking at him so intently she would surely have missed the movement. Her pulse fluttered at the absolute beauty of those lips.

"I owe you," he murmured, even closer now.

Panic trickled through her, slowing her body's instant fight-or-flight reaction to his proximity. Ryan could wake up any moment and start screaming for his mommy—or worse, he could climb out of the crib and toddle onto the porch. That image opened the floodgates of her anxiety.

"I'd like you to leave now, Court." She started to take a step back, but he moved again, stalling her. His hand came up to her face, and those long, tanned fingers smoothed that forever-errant wisp of hair from her cheek. Warmth spread through her so fast that it made her light-headed. How could a mere touch affect her so?

"I didn't mean to hurt you, Brin." He searched her eyes, looking for forgiveness or maybe just trying to read what he saw there. "I hope you know that."

"We're not talking about the past, remember?" she protested, however shakily.

He swallowed hard. She watched the slow movement of muscle beneath smooth, tanned skin. "Right." He studied her face a moment longer, as if committing to memory the changes time and worry had wrought.

"Goodbye, Court." This time Sabrina stepped away from him. She needed distance. And a new heart. One that wouldn't let Court Brody inside.

"I'll be back," he warned, "and then we'll set things straight."

Sabrina watched him stalk back to his truck. He dropped behind the wheel, and then drove away. She didn't move until he'd disappeared in the direction of town—or more accurately, the militia compound.

"Don't come back, Court," she murmured, her heart sinking. "I can't survive losing you again."

CHAPTER TWO

STILL TIRED FROM yesterday's cleaning frenzy, Sabrina smiled for her son and ruffled his silky brown hair. He gurgled and cooed, his gray eyes sparkling as he bounced up and down in anticipation of his mother scooping him up.

"Sorry, sweetie, Mommy has something she has to do this morning." She hated to leave him, but she sure couldn't take him with her to the compound.

Ryan protested, jerking against the brightly colored sides of his playpen.

"I don't like the idea of you going out to that place, Sabrina," Mrs. Cartwright said softly, her aged voice as heavy with worry as her faded blue eyes. "I've heard some pretty disturbing rumors about what they're doing out there."

Sabrina folded her arms over her middle and turned away from the concerned gaze that studied her too closely. She'd known Mrs. Cartwright forever, and she trusted her completely. "I don't know what else to do. They've offered to let me help with home schooling some of the younger children." She shrugged. "It's just for a couple of hours a day."

The older woman moved to her side and ruffled

Ryan's hair as Sabrina had only moments ago. He babbled his approval at the attention. "But you already work too hard," Mrs. Cartwright argued. "You don't need another job." She shook her head and gazed up at Sabrina. "Especially not at that place and one that doesn't pay. You should be with your son."

A weary sigh slipped past Sabrina's lips. How could she explain that she didn't have a choice in the matter? "It's the only way I have of keeping an eye on Charlie. He won't listen to anything I say anymore."

"He's a good boy, Sabrina," Mrs. Cartwright protested. "He's just missing a father figure in his life. He'll come around."

Sabrina scrubbed a hand over her face and blinked back the tears that stung her eyes. "I know. But, God, couldn't he have looked anywhere but to Neely?" She prayed that her elderly friend was right and that Charlie would come around…soon.

"Lots of folks considerably older than Charlie are following the man." Mrs. Cartwright sighed, the effort heaving from her thin chest. "Joshua Neely seems to have what they're looking for, as frightening as that sounds."

Instantly, Court sprang to Sabrina's mind. How could he fall for a guy like Neely? It just didn't make sense to her, no matter what his excuse. Sabrina had a sneaking suspicion that Court wasn't being completely honest with her. How could he just up and walk away from the FBI? He had been in love with the whole damned superagent mystique. He sure hadn't been in love with her. She suppressed the old hurt that accompanied that thought.

Her gaze drifted down to Ryan. Having given up on

his mommy rescuing him from his red-and-blue prison, he now sat playing with his spongy stacking blocks. Court may have broken her heart, but he had given her the one thing that got her through each day—her son. His birth had coincided with the realization that hard financial times were ahead, not to mention Charlie's plunge into adolescence and his subsequent rebellious behavior.

Ryan made life bearable. She would protect him from the hurtful games adults played. No one—not even Court—would hurt her son. Sabrina would see to that.

"I have to get going." Sabrina bent down and dropped a kiss on her baby's sweet head. She forced a smile for her elderly friend. "I'll be back around lunchtime."

Mrs. Cartwright followed Sabrina to the door. "Be careful, Sabrina." She smoothed a hand over the tight bun she'd twisted her gray tresses into. "I worry about you, you know."

Taller than most women, Sabrina leaned down and gave Mrs. Cartwright a quick hug. "I'll be fine. Don't worry about me, I'm tougher than I look. Just take good care of my little boy." Besides, Sabrina didn't add, with her long legs she could probably outrun most of the men she knew—Joshua Neely and his cohorts included.

Mrs. Cartwright waved goodbye from the door as Sabrina backed away from the house. She drove to the end of the dirt road that served as a driveway to the Cartwright place and then pointed her old truck in the direction of the militia compound. Sabrina glanced at her reflection in the rearview mirror. How long had it been since she had bothered with makeup? Two years, an impatient voice reminded her.

"You're pathetic, Korbett," she accused.

Not only had she dabbed on a touch of makeup, she'd taken the time to French-braid her hair. A haphazard ponytail was her usual hairdo. Sabrina huffed her disgust. To make matters worse she had scrounged around until she found her best pair of jeans and her one almost-new blouse she saved for wearing to Ryan's pediatrician appointments.

She scowled at the road before her. So what was wrong with wanting to look her best? After all, she was going to a job of sorts. There would be other women there who would probably be dressed similarly. Just because she took a little more care than usual today didn't mean she'd done it for Court.

"Yeah, right," she muttered.

Truly pathetic.

Sabrina braked to a stop in front of the gate leading to the compound. She kept her gaze straight ahead as the armed guard—Jed Markham, a man she had known her entire life—inspected her truck inside and out. She clenched her teeth at the fury that unfurled inside her. A twelve-foot-high chain-link fence, topped with concertina wire, protected the compound from intruders. Four manned observation towers stood in strategic locations. The place looked like a military base prepared for war. The hard-core followers, like the one circling her old truck now, even wore military garb.

Jed waved an arm and the gate slowly opened in front of her. "You can pass," he barked.

"Didn't find anything suspicious, huh?" Sabrina

asked, baiting him sweetly, with a matching sugary smile. "I guess I hid that bomb better than I thought."

Jed simply glared at her as he worked the wad of tobacco in his mouth until he could spit.

Sabrina rolled her eyes and drove on through the gate. She parked near the meeting hall, which also held the two classrooms, and climbed out into the brisk morning air. Fall was right around the corner. Then winter would be here before she knew it. She dreaded the bad weather to come. If Charlie didn't come back home to help her—she would not think that way. She would win him back…somehow. She had to make him see that men like Neely were only taking advantage of the good intentions of the people here. She just hoped she wouldn't be too late.

"Morning, Sabrina," Lorie Beecham called out as Sabrina made her way into the classroom. "We're sure glad to have you. We've got two new students this morning."

Sabrina surveyed the dozen or so children in the room. How could people bring their innocent children to a place like this? She resisted the urge to shiver. Someone had to stop Neely before something bad happened.

But who?

Her thoughts went automatically to Court. She forced his image from her mind. She had to remember that he was a part of this now….

He was one of them.

COURT APPRAISED Joshua Neely's office as he waited for the man to show up for their scheduled meeting. The young man who served as Neely's personal assistant or secretary of sorts had insisted that Court have a seat and wait since Neely was expected back momentarily. But Court didn't want to sit. Instead, he paced, surveying Neely's framed mementos.

Floor-to-ceiling bookcases lined one wall. Law books filled most of the shelves. According to the intelligence Court had on Neely, the man held a degree in political science as well as law. The office furnishings were an odd blend of typical middle-management style and more elegant oak pieces probably donated by enamored followers. The only disturbing elements were the newspaper clippings of high profile cases between other militia groups and the federal authorities, framed and hanging on nearly every available inch of wall space. Then there were the banners proclaiming Neely's position on the law of the land. True Freedom Lies in the Heart of the Sons and Daughters of this Great Land. We Shall End the Oppression.

Court caught himself before he shook his head. Between the rally and a mostly sleepless night in the barracks with a group of particularly fervent followers, he was edgy this morning. Two weeks of hanging out at the Watering Hole, a hangout where one or more militia members could always be found, had finally paid off yesterday. Court moved back to the desk and dropped into one of the available chairs. The undertones in Neely's speech at the rally and the intense reaction of those present had seriously unsettled Court. This wasn't the first group of this nature he had investigated, but this one was certainly the most enthusiastic. Yet, it was something more that had him so uneasy. Something he couldn't quite put his finger on.

There was nothing wrong with enthusiasm, but it was the man who garnered the reactions that disturbed him, he decided. Court couldn't quite label his suspicions just yet, but a bad scenario was forming in his mind.

Anybody around when that scenario reached fruition would likely be caught in the fallout.

The taste of Sabrina, sweet and warm, abruptly filled his mind, startling Court. The kiss he'd stolen from her had haunted what little sleep he'd managed last night. He had purposely forgotten how pretty she was. Even as a kid, all arms and legs with a honey-brown ponytail that hung to her waist, Sabrina had been too appealing for her own good. She and Court had grown up together on the Double K, and she'd spent most of her days following him around. By age twelve she'd had herself a serious case of hero worship. Only a year older, Court hadn't minded. Even now the sound of her laughter, the memory of the way those dark chocolate eyes twinkled made him want to smile…made him regret.

Court snapped himself from that pointless line of thinking. That was a different life and he wanted no part of that past. Without success, he tried to blink away the image of how she'd looked when she found him at her door. Flushed, her skin glistening with perspiration from the work she'd obviously been doing in the barn. Though she was still tall and thin, there was something different about Sabrina. Court frowned, trying to pinpoint the subtle change. She was softer somehow, but every bit as lean and strong as before. Sabrina Korbett was only a couple of inches shy of his height of six foot two. He smiled at the thought that he'd never known her to be afraid of anyone or anything. Not even when she should have been…afraid of him, that is.

Court passed a hand over his face and swore at his inability to keep his mind off the woman he'd spent half a lifetime trying to forget.

"I hope I haven't kept you waiting too long, Court."

Court pushed to his feet as Joshua Neely, followed by his first lieutenant, entered the office. "No problem, Joshua." He accepted the man's hand and shook it. "I've been reading." Court gestured to the framed newspaper articles.

Neely nodded, his expression grave. "A sad history of the oppression. I fear it will take extreme measures, perhaps even terrorist-type activities to ever make the government understand that we will no longer lie down and allow them to march over us." He indicated the man at his right. "Have you met Thad Ferguson?"

Court extended his hand in Ferguson's direction. "Raymond introduced us last night."

Ferguson squeezed Court's hand in blatant challenge but said nothing. Court smiled and returned the gesture twofold, then released the other man's hand and turned back to Neely. Court felt Ferguson's glare on him for several more tense seconds. If the man wanted a pissing contest, Court was ready to oblige.

"Please, make yourselves comfortable, gentlemen." Seemingly oblivious to the tension between the two men, Neely settled into the high-backed swivel chair behind his desk. "We need to get to know one another a little better."

Adrenaline stung as it flowed swiftly through Court's

veins, putting him on alert. Forcing his tense muscles to relax, he settled back into his chair. "What would you like to know that you don't already?" No point in beating around the bush. Neely had questions. Court could only hope that his cover remained intact.

"I spoke to Mr. Cornelius in Richmond," Neely began, then rested his elbows on his desk and steepled his fingers.

Slipping into anti-interrogation mode, Court forced all thought from his mind. He leveled his gaze on Neely's. "Has Mrs. Cornelius recovered from her bout with pneumonia?"

Neely smiled. "Fully." He leaned back into his chair, his hands clasped in front of him. "Mr. Cornelius was most impressed with your horseman talents…as well as your marksman skill." Neely lifted one dark brow. "He raved about your ability to size up a situation and take quick, decisive action. Said he'd never seen anyone track the way you could. Apparently the two of you went hunting quite regularly."

"As often as possible," Court agreed noncommittally. Elmo Cornelius was an uncle to a fellow agent Court had worked with for years. Elmo had jumped at the chance to play a part in Court's cover.

"Mr. Cornelius was rather distressed with your sudden decision to leave his employment. He's still looking for a worthy replacement," Neely offered, his gaze expectant.

"After the Falls Meadow incident, things changed," Court explained. "I realized when the feds murdered those folks for simply standing up against unfair gun control that I had to do something. I hadn't forgotten the ideals of the Sons and Daughters, and I felt compelled to come home to my roots. To stand up for what was right."

Neely glanced at the framed article that retold, from the media's point of view, the bloodbath of Falls Meadow, Virginia. The feds were the bad guys as usual. No one cared that antigovernment elements were springing up everywhere these days. Most were harmless, but some represented a danger to themselves and the surrounding community. It was those few who made it tough for everybody. The unfortunate incident at Falls Meadow had coincided time and locationwise for Court's cover.

"You want to fight back? To avenge the wrong done to those people?" Neely prodded.

Court pinned him with a look that alluded to much but gave nothing conclusive. "I want to make a difference."

One of those practiced smiles spread across Neely's face. "You feel it, too, don't you, Court?" He nodded his approval. "I thought as much. I can see it in your eyes."

"I feel very strongly." *About bringing you down,* Court added silently. Every instinct warned him that Neely was dangerous. A snake in the grass, Court decided, coiled up and hissing a tune that mesmerized its victims.

"We need you, Court," Neely said with quiet determination. "These people need you. You've received the calling, and I'd like the honor of guiding your journey. You have something special to offer us, I can feel it. We invite you to serve our cause in a position of leadership, Court Brody, as destiny has so clearly chosen."

"I'm ready." Court stood and stretched out his hand to the man behind the desk. "I accept your invitation, Joshua."

Neely rose, clasped Court's hand and shook it firmly. "Amen, Brother Brody, welcome to our cause."

AFTER A MORE EXTENDED TOUR of the facilities the compound offered and two and one-half hours on the firing range to observe training procedures, Court lagged behind the rest as they headed toward the dining hall. Yet another surprise had awaited him on the firing range, a large number of recruits were young boys. Most were accompanied by their fathers, some were with their mothers. He knew he shouldn't be surprised by the sheer number of kids involved, but he was just the same. It rattled him clear to his bones. Those kids could have been him and his brothers.

Stalling in the middle of the quadrangle, Court surveyed his militant surroundings. This was no place for children. The idea of any of the children he'd seen today being hurt or worse made him sick to his stomach. He had to put a stop to Neely. Whether the man was connected to the Black Order, a multi-national terrorist group, or not, Neely was a danger to these people. Court felt pretty confident that these folks only wanted to stand up for their beliefs.

"Court! Court Brody!"

Court whipped toward the adolescent voice that called out to him. A boy, maybe thirteen or fourteen, with brown hair clipped high and tight, and dressed in camouflage fatigues, sprinted in Court's direction.

Did he know this kid? Grinning widely, the boy skidded to a stop directly in front of him.

"I'll betcha don't remember me, do ya, Court?" His

brown eyes twinkled, vaguely familiar. A sprinkling of freckles fanned over his nose and cheeks.

One corner of Court's mouth quirked up at the kid's unabashed enthusiasm. "You got me." He chucked the boy's shoulder…the same way he used to do to Sabrina when they were kids. "Want to give me a clue?"

"I'm Charlie Korbett, Sabrina's brother," he replied, as if Court should have known without any reminders. "I remember you from the funeral. My sister told me all about you. She said y'all used to ride horses, climb trees and do all kinds of things together."

A twinge of unease pricked Court. Had Sabrina told her kid brother about the FBI? It sounded as if she'd told him most everything else. He snapped his fingers and made a sound of disbelief. "Man, I should have known that. I guess you've just gotten so grown up that I didn't recognize you. And I have been gone a long time."

"Yeah, I know," Charlie put in quickly. "Sabrina told me you were off doing some important job."

Court tensed. "She told you about that, huh?"

Charlie nodded with the same vigor that he spoke. "Uh-huh. But she doesn't talk much about you anymore." His expression clouded. "Not since the funeral."

One by one Court's muscles relaxed from their fight-or-flight stance. "It's good to see you again, Charlie."

His freckled face brightened. "I'm glad you're here, Court. Maybe you can get Sabrina off my back."

Across the quadrangle Sabrina stopped dead still. Her worst fears were realized when she saw Charlie talking to Court. She hadn't had a moment alone with her brother to warn him to keep his mouth shut about

Ryan. And now it was probably too late. She had to think of something and do it—fast.

Charlie grinned up at Court, his face beaming with pride.

Really fast.

"Charlie Korbett," Sabrina said in her sternest voice as she marched toward the two. "Why didn't you come home last night?" She refused to look at Court. She'd seen far too much of him yesterday. Enough to keep her hot and bothered all night long. Enough to make her downright steamy today.

Charlie glared at her, a flush rushing up his neck and across his cheeks. She'd embarrassed him. Sabrina swore silently. That sure wouldn't win her any points with her little brother. But keeping her secret was the most important thing at the moment.

"What do you care?" He hurled the words at her like missiles intended to wound. He hit the mark.

"Charlie, I—"

"You don't care about anything but Ryan. Why don't you just leave me alone."

Fear paralyzing her, Sabrina could only watch as Charlie stormed away, his long, skinny legs eating up the ground. He'd mentioned Ryan. She tried to breathe, but the air wouldn't flow into her starved lungs.

"Teenagers are like that," Court offered, his calm, whiskey-smooth voice vanquishing the ugly, screaming silence left by Charlie's abrupt departure. "They always blow up at the people they love most."

Sabrina all but staggered with the burst of oxygen that suddenly filled her chest. She jerked with the reality that Charlie had given away her secret. The ground seemed to shift beneath her feet. Her stomach roiled. Court would ask about Ryan next.

"Brin, are you all right?" Court was right in front of her now, steadying her swaying form.

She looked into those gray eyes staring at her with such concern from beneath the brim of his hat and something akin to a sucker punch jarred her to the core. Awareness glittered in those silvery depths, but no questions, no accusations. Relief, so profound, washed over her that she swayed again. He hadn't picked up on Charlie's comment.

Thank God.

"I'm fine." She pulled out of his hold. Warmth simmered where his palms had closed over her bare flesh. "I have to find Charlie." She started to go, but Court stayed her, the strong fingers of his hand once more curling around her arm. She didn't want to feel this.

"Let him go," he urged softly. "He's angry right now. He needs to cool off. I can talk to him, if you'd like."

Sabrina's jaw fell slack. The very idea. "You never hung around long enough before to help out, why bother now?" Damn. She hadn't meant to say that.

Nevertheless, like Charlie, her words hit their mark. Court's wince was hardly more than a facial tic, but she saw it. How could she have said those precise words? They were steeped with far too much of what she felt deep inside, they gave away too much.

"You're right," he admitted. "I didn't hang around, but I never promised you I would."

She had to get away from him. They didn't need to have this discussion. Not now. Not ever.

"Let me go, Court," she demanded. "I have to find my brother. Believe it or not, some people take their personal responsibilities seriously."

His fingers tightened insistently as he pulled her closer, but it was the lead in his eyes that made her pulse leap with an inkling of trepidation.

"I would never have guessed you for one to hold a grudge," Court rasped tightly. A muscle flexed in his jaw. "I don't recall twisting your arm that night. After all, I had just buried my mother. You came to me, remember? And we were both adults. It wasn't like the first time when we were just kids."

Fury swept through Sabrina at his words. How dare he break it down to such a simple level! There was absolutely nothing simple about what happened that night.

"You needed me, and I was there," she managed to grind out, despite the trembling now rampant in her body. She sucked in a harsh breath and tried to calm the equal measures of anger and sexual awareness twisting inside her. How could she still be so drawn to him?

He pressed her with a glare that wilted the last of the starch from her shaky bravado. "You don't think I appreciate that you were there for me that night, Brin, is that the problem here?"

She jerked against his hold one more time, her fury renewing itself, shoring up her resolve, at his inability to see what was so very clear. "Have you ever thought that maybe a time came when I needed you, and you weren't anywhere around for me?"

He closed his eyes. He was so close that his warm breath feathered across her lips. Sabrina shivered in spite of herself. Why had she said that? She had to get away from him before she said too much.

His lids fluttered open and that silvery gaze was cluttered with what looked like regret. "What do you want me to say, Brin? I did what I had to do. I couldn't stay. I thought you, of all people, understood that?"

"Let me go, Court." Sabrina stumbled back a step at the intensity of the remorse in his eyes. She didn't want to see it. She wanted to keep believing that he hadn't cared and still didn't. It was the only way she could justify her own actions. "Just let me go."

"We need to set things straight between us, Brin." He shook his head. "I don't want to hurt you."

Too late.

She yanked her arm free of his touch. "Stay away from me," she warned. "And stay away from my brother."

He cocked one sandy-brown brow. "That'll be pretty difficult since you keep showing up around here and your brother seems to be a part of the movement," he suggested with that old Court confidence. His stance had already eased into that sensual, predatory male posture that had always made her heart pound in her rib cage. Just like it did now.

"I'm helping with the children," she said when she found her voice. "They needed another teacher. And my brother is a kid, he doesn't realize what he's doing."

"Then, I suppose we'll be seeing a lot of each other."

Sabrina swallowed and backed away another step. "Don't think you can pick up right where you left off, Court Brody," she warned, ire surging through her. "I'm not the foolish girl I used to be."

One side of his mouth hitched up in a heart-stopping, sexy gesture. "I never thought you were," he assured her in that low, husky voice that made her insides quiver.

"I have a life now…one that doesn't include you," she retorted, aiming for a direct hit to his enlarged ego. He ignored it.

A frown line suddenly formed between his eyebrows as if he'd just remembered something important. "By the way, who's Ryan?"

CHAPTER THREE

COURT'S QUESTION reverberated through her, rocking her already crumbling resolve. Sabrina grappled for an answer that would satisfy his mounting curiosity. The longer he waited, searching her face, reading the uncertainty she couldn't hide, the more suspicious he grew.

A sudden jolt of fury fueled her courage. "He's none of your business," she snapped. "In fact, nothing about me is any of your damned business anymore, and you'd better get that notion through your thick skull, Brody."

His silvery gaze narrowed, then darkened with irritation. "Fine. If that's the way you want it, that's the way it'll be. I just thought we could be friends."

Friends? The blast of anger she experienced moments before erupted into blazing flames of raging emotion inside her, tightening her throat and chest, sending adrenaline pumping through her veins. He wanted to be friends? He'd stolen her heart so long ago that she had forgotten what it felt like to have any control whatsoever over her own desires or dreams. Then, when it appeared the rest of her life was determined to fall completely apart around her, he waltzed back into town nine years after leaving her behind and took what her foolish heart openly offered just as if he had never left at all. Two years passed without another single word, and now he wanted to be friends.

"Friends like you I don't need." Sabrina spun away from his intense glare and practically sprinted back to the sanctuary of the classroom. Her heart slammed mercilessly against the aching wall of her chest. That was too close…way, way too close.

Once inside the meeting hall door, she sagged against the wall and attempted to catch her fleeing breath. She had to find a way to avoid Court altogether. Just being near him shook her, tied her up in knots so that she couldn't think straight. She just couldn't deal with another of these high intensity face-offs.

She took another deep, calming breath. She needed to do two things to protect her son and herself. Her plan was simple, she would avoid Court Brody at all costs, and she had to make sure Charlie never mentioned Ryan to him again. That in itself would be no small feat. Charlie questioned everything she said these days. More often than not he argued against whatever she decided. But she had no choice. She had to make him see, without telling him the reason, that Court could never find out about Ryan.

Satisfied now that she had a plan, Sabrina pushed away from the wall and walked toward the classroom to the left of the main hall. As she entered the room, she produced a smile for the dozen sets of curious eyes that greeted her. This was where she had to focus her attention. Whatever happened within the walls of this compound, whatever insanity Joshua Neely had planned, Sabrina had to find a way to protect these children and her independence-seeking brother.

She glanced at the two solemn-faced teachers hovering over Neely's provided lesson plans. No one else here recognized the truth of the matter. But Sabrina saw it as clearly as day—Joshua Neely was a wolf wearing sheep's clothing—she surveyed the room again—and these little lambs were his prey.

COURT STOOD IN THE MIDDLE of the quadrangle, barely registering the comings and goings of those around him. He scrubbed a hand over his face and tried to sort the tangle of reactions twisting inside him.

There was another man in Sabrina's life. Court swallowed, the movement restricted by the emotion clamped around his throat. He had anticipated that, hadn't he? Hadn't he fully expected her to be married and maybe have a kid by now? Just because he'd come home two years ago, after nine years of living away, and had found Sabrina still single and ready to fall once more into his arms didn't mean that she would be still waiting.

Court released a long, frustrated breath. Deep down, he admitted, that's exactly what he had expected. Oh, he could fool himself by saying that he hadn't really anticipated seeing her. Or that he didn't even know for sure that she was still around the area. But they would be lies.

In the deepest recesses of his soul he had known she would be here, still running the ranch her daddy had left her. Still holding some power over his heart that he couldn't quite label...or *wouldn't* label. No matter how far away or how fast he ran, something about Sabrina kept a part of him forever attached to this place. The place he never wanted to see again, the place where he'd spent his teen years restless and impatient. The place he'd been ready to watch fade in the rearview mirror of the first vehicle he'd ever owned for far too long before the wish became a reality. The day he'd finished paying for that old Ford truck, he'd kissed his mother goodbye and left Montana without ever looking back, other than the occasional brief visit.

Court cursed himself for dredging up and overanalyzing ancient history. He didn't belong here anymore, no matter what that small part of him still connected on some level to Sabrina said. When this assignment was over, he would leave, and this time he wouldn't be back. Once Montana Confidential was up and running full steam, there wouldn't be any need for a guy like him. An ex-Montana boy. Next time anything went down in the Treasure State, the Bureau would just have to send some other sucker. With the Confidential boys in place, there would be no excuse that they needed someone familiar with the people and the landscape.

"Court!"

Court turned around to find Raymond Green doubletiming it in his direction. "Yo, Raymond, what's up?" He manufactured a smile of greeting for the zealous man.

"Joshua wants to see you in the hole."

Court frowned. "The hole?"

Raymond grinned, excitement gleaming in his eyes. "Come on, I'll show you the way."

The hole was an apt description, Court decided, as he stared into the dimly lit tunnel before him. Raymond had escorted Court into the rear of the training center and down a flight of stairs to the basement, then through a well-stocked storm shelter. Neely was ready for anything, Court decided upon observing the array of stored goods before his eyes. At the far side of the shelter a section of ingenious false storage shelves were pulled away from the wall to reveal a horizontal tunnel that led slightly downward and did a ninety-degree angle to disappear out of sight. Fluorescent lights, spaced too far apart for Court's liking, provided the dim illumination.

"This way." Raymond gestured for Court to precede him. Raymond pulled the well-camouflaged door shut behind them, lessening the already low light.

Court remained calm, but his senses were on full-scale alert just in case this was some sort of setup. His lawman instincts had never failed him before, he hoped they weren't about to now. "Well, this is interesting," he noted aloud for his escort's benefit.

"You ain't seen nothing yet," Raymond assured him. The man's anticipation was palpable.

As Court followed Raymond down the few steps and to the left, he absorbed as many details as possible in the poor lighting. The walls were concrete, like a vault. The corridor that lay before them was maybe fifty feet long. Court could just make out two doors on the right, twenty or thirty feet apart. There appeared to be only one door on the left side of the corridor.

Raymond stopped at the first door they reached, the one on the left. He unlocked and opened it. The heavy steel door made a sound that wasn't quite a groan but something on that order when it swung inward. The eerie sound triggered an uneasy feeling deep in Court's gut. The hair on the back of his neck stood on end and his pulse reacted instantly to a surge of adrenaline.

"This is the ammo room."

Court looked from Raymond to the open door and back. "I thought the ammo room was upstairs."

"This is the *real* ammo room."

When Court stepped inside the surprisingly large room he knew exactly what his new best friend meant. Court surveyed the room and let go a low whistle that garnered an I-told-you-so look and a chuckle from Raymond. The only place Court had ever seen a stockpile of weapons and ammo like this was at the bust of a heavy-duty arms dealer.

"Oh, yeah," Court agreed, "this is real, all right." Too damned real.

"I'm tellin' you, buddy, Joshua's got everything we need." Raymond closed and locked the heavy door once Court was back in the corridor. "And he's got way bigger plans than this." He jerked his head toward the ammo-room door. "Way bigger. With the Order's help he's gonna show those bastards running this country where the power is, and it ain't in Helena or D.C., my friend."

The *Order?* Court's pulse reacted as his senses moved to a new level. Raymond definitely meant the Black Order. Court adopted his most unsuspecting expression. "Damn, buddy, I had no idea we had this much power. This is incredible."

Raymond ushered him toward the next door. "I'll show you 'incredible.'"

The first door on the right led to a high-tech communications center that rivaled the one at the Lonesome

Pony ranch in state-of-the-art hardware, but this one was considerably larger. So, Court decided, now he knew the reason for the two satellite dishes located behind the building. Upon first inspection it would appear that they were used to support the small communications room in the meeting hall and for video-conferencing of training classes in this building, but that wasn't the case at all.

Two technicians monitored the equipment, paying little or no attention to the intrusion. The man was clever, Court had to give him that. Joshua Neely was networking on a level that no one would ever suspect. This wasn't just some little half-baked setup he had going here…this was the whole enchilada. Joshua Neely had much more going on than anyone, even Court, had first suspected.

"Now for the grand finale," Raymond announced as they walked back into the corridor.

"What's at the end of the tunnel?" Court asked, halting Raymond's tour to peer toward the far end of the passage. Now that he was closer, he could see that the corridor took another hard left.

"That leads to the escape tunnel," Raymond explained. "If we're ever in danger of being overrun by the feds, we can escape to safety. It comes out deep in the mountains."

Court nodded. "Cool."

"Damn right." Raymond ushered Court to the last door on the right. "Now, the one we've been waiting for."

Once they stepped inside the final doorway, Court stood, stunned for several seconds. The room was white—walls, ceiling, floor. So white and so brightly lit that it took a moment or two for his eyes to adjust. In stark contrast to the whiteness, a round, gleaming black conference table occupied the center of the room. Nearly a dozen men were seated around it, leaving two empty chairs of the same polished ebony as the table. Joshua Neely's larger, more thronelike chair sat in the designated place of honor.

Neely stood. "Welcome, Court." He indicated those seated around the table with a sweeping motion of his right arm. "These are my leaders, my lieutenants."

Court nodded first to Neely, then surveyed those seated. Ferguson and a few of the others he recognized, Potts and Beecham. One of the empty seats was to Neely's immediate left, the other on Ferguson's right. The men seated didn't bother to rise, they merely stared at Court, measuring and considering. Raymond hustled around the table and sat down in the empty chair beside Ferguson, leaving Court standing alone outside the strange dark circle.

The Knights of the Round Table. The crazy notion came out of nowhere. Court resisted the urge to laugh out loud at the ridiculous thought. He started to speak, but one of the men, Greg Potts, if Court remembered correctly, rose from his chair, cutting off his question. He'd noticed the quiet, soft-spoken man before. As yet, Court hadn't figured out just what his expertise was. But if he worked this closely with Neely, Potts had something on the ball. Potts walked deliberately to Court and embraced him.

"Brother," he said before releasing Court.

Court blinked, uncertain what was expected of him. "Brother," he replied hesitantly.

One by one, each of those seated followed suit. Ferguson was the last to approach Court. The embrace as well as the greeting was forced. This man, Court knew at that instant, would be his most powerful enemy. He'd been getting bad vibes from him since day one.

When Ferguson would have backed away, Court drew him closer. "Brother," he murmured fervently.

Ferguson tensed, fury in his gaze when he drew back. The gauntlet was down now. Court watched Ferguson retreat to his station on Neely's right. Keep your friends close, but your enemies closer, Court reminded himself silently. That would keep both of them out of trouble. Court restrained the smile of secret amusement that twitched one corner of his mouth.

"Brother Brody," Neely announced, drawing Court's attention to the one remaining person in the room who had not participated in the little ceremony.

"Come forward, brother," Neely instructed.

With the others watching his every step, Court moved toward Neely. They'd already given him one induction last night. What was this all about? Maybe Neely just enjoyed the pomp and circumstance of it all.

"Last night we welcomed you to our brotherhood," Neely began as if reading Court's mind. "Today, brother—" he placed a hand on Court's shoulder "—we welcome you into the ranks of our leaders." He gestured to the vacant chair at his left. "Take your place of honor among those who, like you, possess the special gift. The calling."

Court sank into the designated chair, his gaze fixed on Neely's. Something in that pale blue gaze sent a chill straight through him.

"Now, Brother Brody, select your challenger," Neely directed.

"Challenger?" Court schooled his expression so as not to show his unease or his surprise. Whatever test Neely had in mind, he would deal with it. Anything to maintain his cover. But it was always an advantage to know what "it" was.

Neely nodded. "Each new lieutenant must endure the challenge, a simple survival test, in order for us to know that he is pure of heart and thought. You will select the man from among these pure ones before you, and that one will be your challenger." Neely looked from one attentive face to the other. "At midnight on this night you will be blindfolded and taken deep into the wilderness. Your challenger will be in pursuit at half past the hour. The men in this room are highly trained, as I'm sure you well know. If you survive until dawn, you will remain in this place of honor."

Anticipation of the unexpected battle instantly sharpened Court's senses. He scanned the men around the table. Raymond would probably be his wisest choice. Though Raymond was a good marksman, and a more-than-competent opponent in hand-to-hand combat, Court was well enough acquainted with the man to know his weaknesses.

"One month has passed since this circle was complete," Neely continued, no doubt loving the sound of his own voice. "It is time we replaced our fallen warrior. Make your decision and we shall be done with formalities."

Court had a pretty good idea that the so-called fallen warrior was the man charged with killing a Livingston businessman last month. Running for political office, the businessman spoke out vehemently against the militia, making himself a target. The shooter had turned the gun on himself when threatened with capture. To prevent interrogation, no doubt, thus protecting Neely. Of course, there was no way to prove whether the man had acted on his own or under orders from his esteemed leader.

Whatever the case, Court now had the opportunity to slip into the upper echelon. All he had to do was pass Neely's little test. Court studied those seated around the table a moment longer. If he selected Raymond, Neely would know he had taken the easy way out. This was a test, and Court had to prove his worthiness. Finally, his gaze settled onto the man he would seriously enjoy taking down a notch or two. "Brother Ferguson is my choice," he announced.

Ferguson smiled, a gesture rich with malice and anticipation. "It will be my pleasure, Brother Brody."

"Excellent choice, Brother Brody," Neely commented, obviously pleased. "I am certain that you will prove an outstanding lieutenant."

SABRINA CLOSED ONE EYE and focused on the target. She pulled the trigger and hit a little to the left of the outermost circle of the bull's eye. She swore. She could do better than that. Her father had taught her how to handle a rifle when she was only twelve years old. Just as she had taught Charlie. Frustrated, she jerked off the ear protection and swiped the perspiration from her brow.

She considered the requirement for teachers to participate in basic combat training pretty stupid. She was only here to keep an eye on her brother and to help the children. Leaving her son with Mrs. Cartwright and coming here for *this* wasn't exactly what she'd had in mind. She frowned, tired and irritated. Then again, maybe she did need to know more about how to defend those children as well as her brother. Though she was a pretty good shot, she could be better. And it might just save Charlie's life. As well as her own.

Determined to try harder, Sabrina tossed the annoying ear protection to the ground and assumed the firing position once more. She zeroed in on the center of the bull's eye. Her finger snugged up to the trigger—

A hand suddenly pushed her left elbow a bit higher. Before she could look up and see who'd adjusted her stance, a strong arm snaked around her middle and pulled her against a hard male body. She gasped, startled. A big foot kicked hers farther apart, forcing her to lean into the wall of muscle now wrapped around her.

"Your feet need to be shoulder-width apart," an all-too familiar voice informed her.

Court.

Her traitorous body reacted instantly to the feel of him pressed along her backside. Snapping her composure into place, she tried to pull away.

"What the hell are you doing? Let me go!"

"Don't make a scene, Brin," he murmured against her hair. "You'll make people suspicious."

She stilled. He was right. Though she didn't fully understand how she knew, she did. "Take your hands off me," she hissed for his ears only.

His arm tightened around her, grinding her bottom into his hardening arousal. Sabrina stifled another startled gasp. She wasn't the only one reacting here. The feel of him uncoiled fingers of warmth in her middle that reached outward, heating her all the way to her skin.

"Why are you doing this?"

"Aim your weapon," he ordered, his breath warm against her cheek.

Sabrina obeyed. She could feel his heart pounding as hard as her own. She resisted the urge to close her eyes and simply revel in the clean, masculine scent that folded around her, to sag against the strength of his muscular frame.

"Keep your elbows up."

His voice was rougher, huskier; his body harder. However foolish it was, a pleased smile lifted the corners of her mouth. Determined to prove herself, she took aim and fired, hitting well within the rings of the bull's eye, if not dead center. Struck with sudden wicked inspiration, she shifted her hips a bit. A groan wrenched from his throat. Desire thrilled through her at the sound.

Court's wide palm pressed into her belly, holding her still. "You're playing with fire, Brin," he warned, his lips moving against the sensitive skin near her ear. "And you might just get burned."

"You're the one with the hard-on, Brody," she returned flippantly. "Not me." She readied her rifle once more, proud of herself for the witty comeback.

He reached to adjust her arm, purposely brushing her breast, then drew his hand away so slowly that his fingers slid over her nipple, testing the tightly budded peak beneath the thin cotton of her blouse. Her breath stalled in her lungs at the sting of desire that barbed straight to her core.

"Hmm." The sound rumbled from his chest. "I'd say we're about even."

A mixture of hurt, anger and frustration exploded inside her. She dropped her weapon to her side and whipped around in his hold, putting herself nose-to-nose with him.

"Why don't you just leave me alone, Brody?" She almost jerked back at the feel of his hard arousal pressed against her belly, but she held her ground. The heated blood rushing through her veins roared in her ears, made her body tingle, made her skin burn, made her want to surrender to the power he held over her…still. He felt so strong and steady. But he wasn't. He would only leave her again. Just like before. And she had to protect Ryan from the kind of pain she had endured. Tears welled in her eyes.

He studied her for a moment, his gaze burning with the same desire and want that whirled inside her, beneath all the other mixed-up emotions. How could she feel this way about him? How could she want him so? Need him so desperately? She was tired, that's all. Tired of handling the crushing burdens of her slowly unraveling life alone. But Court was not the answer to her prayers. She knew that if she knew nothing else. He would leave her behind again.

"Be careful, Brin," he murmured. "I understand your need to see after your brother, but there's a lot of danger here, things you can't possibly know." He inclined his head, forcing her to keep eye contact. "I don't want you to get hurt. You need to be extremely cautious in what you say and do."

"Thanks for the warning." She jerked out of his hold, pivoted and sauntered away. She would not overanalyze the sincerity she saw in those gray eyes. So what if she'd thought she'd seen a smidgen of something else there, too? It was probably nothing more than basic human compassion. The kind you have for a stray dog or injured bird. Court didn't care about her, not really. Whatever his agenda here, it didn't include her. Sabrina was just a nuisance he couldn't avoid.

Well, screw him, she decided. She had to protect her brother and her son. Somehow she would find a way to keep Court Brody at bay. He would not take anything else from her. Someday when Ryan was all grown up, Court would know what she had kept from him. And then they'd be even.

AS COURT SAT IN the darkness only minutes before dawn, he waited out his prey. The hunter had become the hunted. Court's lips twitched with amusement. Ferguson just didn't know it yet. While Court waited, he considered Sabrina and her brother Charlie. He was her reason for hanging around the compound. She wanted to keep her little brother safe. Court could understand that, but this militia group, because of its esteemed leader, was turning out to be a much larger threat than first anticipated. Hanging around the place was definitely not a good idea. But Court couldn't warn Sabrina or Charlie too sternly without the risk of blowing his cover. He would just have to figure out some way to protect the two of them.

But protecting Sabrina was not all he wanted to do. He closed his eyes and cursed his lack of perspective when it came to her. He'd spent years trying to erase her presence from his memory, but nothing ever worked for long. It didn't matter how many relationships he had or how far away from Montana he stayed, she was there…always in his mind. Sabrina was such an integral part of the first nineteen years of his life, that he couldn't seem to evict her. Hell, truth be told, he couldn't even say he wanted to keep trying.

Court's eyes opened wide with that admission. He listened to the night sounds for anything human. His gaze moved up to the patch of wide Montana sky visible through the treetops. A million stars still glimmered in the heavens like diamonds scattered across a black velvet jeweler's bag. His heart lurched at the realization that no matter how far he ran or how long he stayed away, this was still home. This land and the hard work of his youth were the things that made him the man he was today. A flash of memory, his father smiling down at him and ruffling his hair, zinged his conscience. He rarely thought of him. Court tried to pretend that the man and his memory meant nothing to him, that his father alone had caused the heartache and lack of material comforts of his childhood.

But the man was still his father, no matter that he had

made their lives harder with his drinking. He'd had a good heart, if no self-discipline. Besides, would Court have the determination he had today if his father had been different? He pushed away that line of thinking. Both his father and mother were long gone, there was no point in rehashing anyone's mistakes…not even his own. Though he had provided well for his mother until her death, as did his three older brothers, Court hadn't visited her as often as he should have. Despite the fact that she had moved to Livingston after the last of her sons left the ranch, it still bothered him to come back. He had carefully avoided Sabrina and the Double K on those occasions, but then his mother had died and Sabrina had entered his life, however briefly, once more.

She hadn't forgiven him for taking that one night and then walking away. Court supposed he couldn't blame her, but he had a life in D.C. and nothing Montana had to offer, not even Sabrina, was going to hold him back. The assignment had to be top priority. An unexpected hollowness accompanied the motto he lived by. Court tunneled his fingers through his hair. Damn, he missed his hat. Though he rarely wore the blasted thing in the city, it hadn't taken him long to fall back into the habit of wearing it regularly.

No hat, no light and no weapon, discounting the pocketknife he'd been allowed to keep. He'd been dumped out here with basically nothing to protect himself but his wits. But then, that was the point, wasn't it? Neely wanted two things. To ensure Court's worthiness as a soldier, and to test his readiness to die for the cause. If he lacked one or both he would either die out here in the darkness at Ferguson's hand or he would run like hell and never come back.

But Court would do neither. By dawn, he planned to move up a little higher on Neely's food chain. A whisper of fabric against foliage captured his full attention. Ferguson was close. Court had left him a clear-enough trail without being too obvious. He could just imagine the smug expression on the man's face. He likely thought he was moving in for the kill. Court smiled. Well, he had a surprise coming to him.

As Court sat silently waiting, the darkness grayed slowly into predawn light. All the while Ferguson moved in the direction Court had planned. Three steps forward, two back. He circled twice before he realized that he was not going anywhere, only around and around. The snap of a twig to his immediate right alerted Court to the man's frustration level and nearness. Men like Ferguson made few tactical errors. It would likely take him a couple more minutes to realize he'd been had, but Court had no intention of allowing that epiphany to dawn before his strike.

Confusion obviously reigning, muddling his thinking, Ferguson backed one step closer to Court's well-camouflaged position.

One last step.

Now!

Court's arm went around the man's shoulder, the sharp blade of the knife to his throat. "Well, well, Ferguson, you took your sweet time finding me."

The man immediately dropped his weapon and held up his hands in surrender. "Glad to see you survived the challenge, brother," he said tightly, fear and uncertainty coloring his tone.

"Sure, *brother,*" Court retorted. "So, I guess this means no one has to die this morning." Court leaned closer, speaking directly into his ear now. "Unless you'd prefer it differently?" The sun suddenly cleared the horizon, reaching down through the trees in warm streaks of gold obliterating the gray.

"You," he croaked. "You wouldn't dare. You've disarmed me."

Court laughed a humorless sound. "Sure I would." He sighed wearily. "But I won't as long as you pull that radio from your belt and let them know that we're on our way back *together.*" He wasn't about to risk Ferguson attempting one last opportunity to take him out before they reached the rendezvous point.

Ferguson grabbed the radio and depressed the talk button. "We're coming in," he growled.

Raymond's expectant voice crackled from the tiny speaker. "You and Court?" he asked for clarification.

"Yes," Ferguson said reluctantly. "We're both coming in."

CHAPTER FOUR

COURT STARED AT the half-empty bottle of beer on the table before him. He had plenty to do without Austin calling this damned urgent meeting. The afternoon had passed in a blur of activity, mostly associated with familiarizing himself with how Neely's lieutenants operated. Ferguson was still pissed as hell at him, but, the way Court looked at it, the fool was lucky to be alive. A man with fewer morals might have slit Ferguson's throat just to take that smug expression off his face. Ferguson was one of those guys who asked for trouble wherever he went, usually without uttering a word.

But Court wasn't looking for trouble. He wanted to keep as low a profile as possible within the lieutenants' ranks until he got the information he needed. If Neely was working with the Black Order, the Bureau needed to know, as did Daniel Austin and his men. But whether he was or not, Neely had to go down. No man with his kind of ideals should ever garner this much power. He was too dangerous. Instantly a vision of the stark white room with its round black conference table for twelve flickered through his thoughts. The man was clearly a few cards shy of a full deck.

Outside the lieutenants, Court doubted if the people

who followed Neely really understood what he was about. He could thunder with righteousness in his tone and dazzle with lightning in his words, swaying those who were seeking something better. Though he was using the resources around him quite efficiently, too much money was involved for it to come from only local sources. That ammo room and communications center were proof positive. Neely had himself some powerful backers. The kind of support the everyday average member of the militia couldn't possibly comprehend.

Court considered Raymond Green and wondered if the man fully understood what he was helping Neely accomplish with his enthusiasm and knowledge of the locals. Though Raymond was a good soldier, well trained and ready to die for the cause, he was not well educated. And if Court had him pegged right, he wasn't savvy about politics or worldwise in any real respect. He'd found a place that he fit in and likely got the glory he'd yearned for his entire life, and he'd burrowed in for the long haul. Going above and beyond the call of duty.

Too bad he'd nested in a den of snakes. Raymond had led the cheers this morning when Court and Ferguson walked down from that mountain. The embrace Raymond had given him in greeting had been heartfelt. Court appreciated the man's friendship, but wasn't sure what, if anything, he could do to help him out of the mess he'd gotten himself into. Men like Raymond were often the ones who were sacrificed the most when guys like Neely went down for their crimes.

Sabrina pushed into Court's head. Where would she be when the proverbial crap hit the fan? He scrubbed a hand over his face and took a long draw from his beer. She needed his protection as well. Her and her rowdy brother. The kid's exuberance at Court's return to the compound this morning was nothing short of exhilarated. He'd latched onto Court for the rest of the morning's festivities. Then Neely had ordered Court to get some rest. But sleep hadn't come easily, despite the night's adventure.

Every detail of the incredible setup Court had seen in the hidden tunnel replayed over and over in his weary mind. Raymond's words about Neely having way bigger plans echoed even now. With this morning's challenge behind him, Court would be included in Neely's long-term plans. Court had no idea how often they had their strategy meetings, but he felt certain that Neely would keep his men up to speed on a regular basis. Court hoped that he would soon know the charismatic leader's ultimate goal and exactly who was helping him achieve it.

Daniel Austin paused at Court's table, his own long-neck bottle of beer dangling from his fingers. "You Court Brody?" he asked with a nonchalance that would fool anybody watching.

"Depends on who's asking." Court sipped his beer, his own demeanor just as relaxed.

"Well, if you're Brody, I heard you were interested in a job working with horses," Austin offered for the ears of those sitting nearest to Court's table who might have taken note of his appearance.

Court gazed up at him from beneath the brim of his hat. "Maybe. If the pay is right."

Austin took a seat directly across from Court and

plopped his bottle onto the worn wooden tabletop. "The pay's fair if you've got the right experience for the job. What kind of history have you got working with animals? Just so you know, I don't need anyone unless he's prepared to work hard for his pay."

Court leaned forward and lowered his voice so that anyone still interested in listening wouldn't overhear what he was about to say. "I gave you an update on everything I'd learned on the phone. I can't imagine what you'd deem important enough to risk my cover with a face-to-face meeting like this."

"I received some intel that has a definite bearing on your assignment," he returned just as pointedly, though his demeanor remained calm and composed despite Court's insubordinate attitude.

Court eased back into a reclining position and chugged another deep swallow of his beer. He set the bottle down with a thunk and licked his lips. "Oh, yeah? And what would that be?" Court knew Austin didn't want him out of his sight for too long. Austin wanted to make damned sure he didn't get left out of the loop on anything.

A tiny line of annoyance creased Austin's brow at Court's consistently uncooperative attitude. "According to my contacts, a local guy by the name of Benson, who just joined the Sons and Daughters, is feeding info to our Alcohol, Tobacco, and Firearms friends. We think maybe they're planning a raid in the very near future."

"The ATF?"

Austin nodded.

More than attentive now, Court bit back a hot curse. He knew the kind of contacts Austin had, and they went all the way to the top. A sting by another agency was all he needed. A raid could set back whatever Neely had planned for weeks, or worse, it could blow the whole operation wide open. "We can't let that happen. I'm too close to finding out what Neely's really up to. Can you run interference?"

Austin shrugged, turning the bottle round and round between his fingers. "Maybe, but it could take some time to persuade the right person with enough influence to put the ATF's plan on hold. You know those guys aren't going to want to surrender jurisdiction."

"We don't have time."

"No," Austin agreed. "In an operation like this, time is your enemy. The longer you're under, the bigger the chance you'll be made."

Court ran down the names and faces of the guys he'd met. *Benson.* Oh, yeah, he remembered him. A short guy with dark hair, about twenty-five or so. He'd been recruited a couple of days before Court, but it was doubtful that he had any worthwhile information just yet. Benson was just another flunky in Neely's growing army. But he would hear rumors, see signs of activity that contradicted the obvious, and that might be enough to warrant a raid.

"I'll have to give him up," Court said with resignation.

Austin nodded. "That was my thought. It would look too suspicious if he simply suddenly disappeared."

"When was his last meeting with his contact?"

"According to my source, they're supposed to meet here any minute now. That's why I wanted to meet here."

"Good." Court glanced around the dimly lit tavern.

He'd met Raymond here. In the years since Court had left, the Watering Hole had obviously become a favored spot of the militia members and most anything else that crawled out from under a rock. He settled his gaze back on Austin's. "And if Neely insists on killing him?"

"I trust you won't allow that to happen," Austin returned, his words a direct order. "Bring him to me and I'll take care of him."

"I'm glad you have so much faith in my ability to sway Neely's command decisions." Court pushed his empty bottle away. "Remember, I'm the new kid on the block."

Austin stood. "I have complete faith in you." He started to turn away but hesitated. "Is the situation with Sabrina Korbett going to be a problem?"

Court's head shot up at the question. "That's none of your business, Austin." He didn't like the man's contin- ued interest in Sabrina or whatever was or wasn't between the two of them. As long as Court did his job, and he would, his personal life was no concern of Austin's.

"Don't make this personal," Austin warned.

"My work is always personal to me." Court's gaze didn't waver from the one staring down so intently at him. He knew his job, he didn't need anyone, especially not Austin, telling him how to do it. "I don't think I'm the man you need," he added, a little louder for anyone taking notes.

Austin gave him a nod. "I'll let you know if anything else comes up," he said quietly, then turned and walked away.

Court ordered another beer, one he didn't plan to drink, and waited for Benson to show. He hoped like hell he could do what had to be done without getting the man killed.

But the assignment was always top priority.

EXHAUSTED FROM THE DAY'S activities, Sabrina had just gotten Ryan down for the night when her front door burst open. It was Charlie.

"Is something wrong?" Immensely thankful that he was home, she surveyed his lanky body for injury. She couldn't imagine his showing up willingly otherwise. She wilted with relief when she found no indication of his being hurt. She wasn't sure how much more of this she could take.

Ignoring her completely, Charlie stormed up the stairs to his bedroom. Sabrina followed. He fumbled in his closet until he found an old gym bag and tossed it on his bed. Continuing to ignore her, he pulled first one drawer open, then another, taking out what he wanted and tossing the items into the open bag. Her heart pounded faster. He was packing.

"What are you doing?" Fear surged through her. Packing was not good. That could only mean he was leaving, and with no intentions of coming back.

"It doesn't matter," he snapped back. "I can do whatever I want to."

"Charlie, you can't do this." Sabrina tried to pull him around to face her, but he jerked from her touch. Hurt pricked her heart, making her want to cry no matter that she needed desperately to be strong. "The militia is dangerous. I've seen enough to know that what they're doing isn't right. I don't want you there."

"I don't care what you want." Fury blazed in his dark eyes. "I can't stand it here anymore. You don't care about me. All you care about is *Ryan.*" He said her son's name with such hatred that her heart sank at the sound.

Sabrina swallowed the lump that formed in her throat. "That's not true, Charlie, and you know it."

He stuffed a couple more things in his bag. "I have friends in the militia. People who care about *me.*" He thumped his skinny chest for emphasis, and his chin trembled. "Like Ferg and Court."

A new kind of fear seized her. "You don't know Court," she argued. "He's caused trouble for me before."

Charlie glared at her insolently. "I don't believe you. I want to be like Court. He's not like *you,* all stupid and bossy. If there was trouble it had to be your fault."

Sabrina winced at the sharp stabs of pain his words caused, but she knew he didn't really mean them. He was a kid, a teenager. He didn't understand about life yet. He couldn't know the things she had learned, that came only with age.

"I know you don't mean that, Charlie," she countered. "I know you love me."

"I don't!" he cried savagely, tears brimming in his eyes now. "I hate you."

Drawing in a deep breath against the tightness in her chest, Sabrina surveyed the room her little brother had spent every night of his life in until the last one. He no longer cared about the Nintendo game and skateboard she had worked so hard to buy him. The telescope and insect collections were forgotten, as well. The boy-man struggle raged within him and Joshua Neely seemed to be the only one who could channel his fierce emotions.

"I could call the sheriff. You're still a minor under my care and keeping, and I can prevent you from going to the compound," she offered slowly, hesitation weighing her words. This was a last resort. She knew without a doubt how he would react to that sort of control.

His glare grew more hate-filled. "Go ahead, but I'll find a way to run away. I won't listen to you anymore!"

Ryan cried out, interrupting what she would have said next. Sabrina's stomach twisted into a thousand knots of uncertainty. Her son needed her, but she couldn't just let her brother walk away. "Charlie, you—" Another cry echoed up the stairs from her bedroom. "I have to go down and get Ryan." She started toward the door.

"Go ahead! Run to Ryan," Charlie called to her back. "He's all you care about, anyway."

Sabrina turned to face her brother. Tears streamed down his cheeks. He brushed impatiently at them. "I love you, Charlie. You know I do."

He dismissed her words with a wave of his hand and returned to his task of packing.

Sabrina hurried down the stairs and to Ryan's crib. Whispering softly to him, she lifted him into her arms and rushed back to Charlie. He was already down the stairs and striding toward the front door, gym bag in hand. She had to stop him somehow.

"Please don't go back, Charlie," she pleaded. He hesitated, one hand on the doorknob. "We need you. We love you."

"I ain't coming back," he said, his voice quaking.

Sabrina closed her eyes against that harsh reality. Ryan snuggled against her and sighed his own agitation. "Wait," she shouted when Charlie would have opened the door.

He turned back to her, belligerence radiating from him, fueled by his impatience. "What?"

"Swear to me that you won't mention Ryan to Court ever again."

He rolled his eyes and blew out a breath. "Why not?"

"Because I said so," Sabrina snapped, out of patience herself. "Ryan and I are none of Court's business. I don't want him snooping around here and asking questions, that's all. So just don't say anything else."

"Fine." Charlie flung the word at her. "Why would I want to talk about the brat, anyway." He stormed out into the darkness, slamming the door behind him.

Ryan whimpered at the loud sound. Sabrina cuddled him closer, tears rolling down her cheeks. What on earth was she going to do? Why hadn't her mother stayed here and raised Charlie like she was supposed to do? Instead, three years ago, she'd signed her part of the ranch over to Sabrina, gotten married again and moved to Florida, putting the past, Charlie and Sabrina included, behind her. She hardly ever called to check on them. Just more proof that Sabrina couldn't count on anyone but herself. Court's handsome face floated before her eyes but she blinked him away. She couldn't count on him, either. Hadn't she already learned that the hard way? Two times over.

The only person she had to help her was poor old Mrs. Cartwright. What would she do when the elderly woman grew too poorly to see after Ryan? How would

Sabrina get any work done on the ranch then? How would she run after Charlie?

Sabrina dropped into the rocking chair and began the slow, rhythmic motion that would hopefully lull both her and Ryan into sleep. Lord knows, she needed the rest. Please God, she prayed, watch over my little brother. Sabrina was truly at her wit's end.

Court sneaked back into her thoughts as she finally drifted toward sleep. Every instinct urged her to trust him. To ask him for help, but she couldn't risk her heart again, could she? Before that elusive answer came, exhaustion overwhelmed her and Sabrina was asleep.

"YOU'RE CERTAIN THIS MAN with whom you saw Benson speaking was a federal agent?" Sitting behind his desk the next morning and appearing completely relaxed, Neely searched Court's face, looking for the slightest mannerism that might contradict his words.

Court met that analyzing gaze head-on. Neely might not show it, but he was shaken by the possibility. "I'd know a fed anywhere. You can shoot 'em and bury 'em in the same suit."

Five seconds passed before a knowing smile overtook Neely's solemn expression. "So, Brother Brody, what would you suggest we do about this traitor?"

Ferguson piped up, "Joshua, I think we should—"

Neely cut Ferguson off with one uplifted palm.

Court glanced at his opponent briefly, then shifted his gaze back to Neely. Just one more strike against him in Ferguson's already low opinion. "I think Benson should pay for his disloyalty."

Neely considered the answer for a time. "I agree," he said finally. He pinned Court with a look that conveyed a great deal more than any words could. "Under my command, the punishment for disloyalty is death."

Court inwardly tensed. He had expected this, but, still, hearing the sentence announced shook him.

"Brother Brody, you are to take care of the traitor in any way you see fit." Neely hardened his already granite glare. "As long as the job gets done, I have no desire to know the intimate details."

Court stood. "It'll be my pleasure."

"Wait," Neely said, staying his departure. When Court turned back to him, Neely reached into his desk drawer and withdrew a Ruger nine-millimeter handgun. "Use my personal weapon," he suggested. "I will destroy this evil among us through you."

Court nodded and accepted the weapon. "Thank you, Joshua." One final look at Ferguson as he left the room told Court that the man was not only madder than hell, but scared...scared that his position as number-one confidant to Neely was in jeopardy of being usurped. If Court had his way, it would be.

SABRINA READIED the children for playtime. Though the compound didn't provide any of the typical playground equipment, a walk in the fresh air and sun would do them all good. Not to mention it would give her a chance to look around for Charlie. Her chest still ached with the hateful words that had passed between them last night.

However, there was nothing she could do at the

moment but be here for him. She only hoped that her presence would be enough. She was certainly powerless in any other capacity within these secured walls.

Sabrina halted abruptly at the bottom of the steps outside the meeting hall. She blinked and looked again just to be sure that what she thought she was seeing was right. Court was ushering a man to his truck. Maybe twenty or thirty others were standing around watching as if the act had some kind of significance. The other man slumped into the truck on the passenger side and Court closed the door behind him. Sabrina jerked with shocked surprise when she got a glimpse of the weapon Court tucked into the waistband of his jeans.

He'd forced that man into his truck at gunpoint. Her heart sank to her stomach. This couldn't be right. There must be more to this than she knew. Court wouldn't do such a thing. Sabrina quickly ushered the children back into the classroom, then hurried back outside.

"Jed!" Sabrina moved up beside the ever-vigilant soldier.

After spitting a mouthful of tobacco juice and saliva onto the dusty ground, he glared, annoyed, at her. "What is it, woman?"

Sabrina ignored the way he addressed her. She needed information. If she angered him he certainly wouldn't tell her anything. "What's going on?" She nodded toward the truck Court had just climbed into.

"Court's taking care of a traitor." Jed spat again. "That's what happens to those who ain't loyal to the cause." He stared at her with an accusing glare. "I wouldn't be forgetting that if I was you."

She felt the color drain from her face. Jed had to be wrong. Court would never do anything like that. *I want to be like Court.* Charlie's words rang out inside her head. Court couldn't have changed that much. She wouldn't believe it. But she'd seen the gun with her own eyes. Maybe she'd been right not to tell him about Ryan, after all. Every fiber of her being rejected that possibility. She simply could not believe Court had fallen so far.

Sabrina stared at the truck as it lurched forward through the crowd on its way to the gate. Suddenly, as if sensing her eyes on him, Court looked her way. Their gazes locked and something she couldn't quite define passed between them. He turned away first. In guilt? This was the man she had once loved with all her heart…the father of her child. What had happened to change him so?

Who was he now? Sabrina shivered at the answer she didn't want to admit but saw no other way to explain his actions. He was one of them. She surveyed those standing around her, watching Court drive away with the traitor. And, if she couldn't stop him soon, Charlie would become one of them, as well. She shook her head, still struggling with what to feel. She didn't have to figure any of this out, she knew with all her heart that what was happening here was wrong.

Very wrong.

SABRINA DROVE AS FAST as her old truck would go toward home…and Ryan. She still couldn't believe what she had seen with her own eyes. How could Court have become that kind of man? He just couldn't have. She called to mind the night they had spent together two years ago. They had made love twice that night, but in between the kisses and the touching they'd talked. He had told her all about the Bureau, or at least as much as he could. He loved his job, loved D.C. That restless heart of his had finally settled onto something that made him truly happy. If only it could have been her.

She shook that last thought away. She remembered his fervent talk of helping bring felons to justice. What had happened to warp that idealism? Sabrina refused to believe he intended harm to the man he'd driven away with in his truck. There had to be some other explanation for the gun.

There simply had to be.

The fact that Joshua Neely was a very persuasive man niggled at her firm belief in Court. And even she had noticed the quick climb Court had made within the militia ranks. There could be no denying that Court was giving his all to Neely's every command.

But why?

What was it he'd said? *I don't want to talk about the Bureau or D.C. I'm trying to put that behind me.* Something very bad must have happened for him to turn his back on all that he had spoken so enthusiastically of just two years ago. Sabrina rubbed at the ache starting in her right temple. She didn't need anyone else to worry about. She had enough of her own problems. Court would just have to work out his own troubles. But Charlie was so taken with him.

The truck jerked and shuddered, then, with one final

sob, the engine died. Sabrina wrestled it to the side of the road while it was still rolling. She stomped the brake pedal and shoved the old gearshift into Park.

"What now?" She blew out a disgusted burst of air and checked the fuel gauge. It showed a half-full tank. She tapped the glass covering it just to make sure it stayed there. Maybe the gauge had malfunctioned. But it remained square in the middle between the *E* and the *F.* If she had enough fuel, what was the problem?

She opened the door and hopped out. Shoving her hair behind her ears with the impatience bursting inside her, she moved to the front of the vehicle. Though she was no mechanic, she supposed it wouldn't hurt to take a look. With monumental effort, she raised the heavy, ancient hood. The alien structure beneath that stared back at her squashed the last of her hope. What had she expected? She only knew which parts were the radiator, which required the occasional addition of water and the place where she poured the oil when it registered a quart low on the stick, which was frequently. The rest was nothing but a conglomeration of gadgets and metal.

She stepped to the side of the road and stared first in one direction, then the other. Surely someone would come along. She laughed, the sound unfamiliar to her ears. Yeah, someone would come along, all right. Maybe tomorrow.

Determined not to be outdone by a mere truck, she reached inside, grabbed a clip and tucked her hair up out of the way. She rarely wore it down, and she'd chosen today of all days. Walking hadn't gone out of style as far she was concerned. It couldn't be more than six or seven miles to Mrs. Cartwright's place. She'd surely make it by dark.

Just as Sabrina headed in the direction of home, she heard a vehicle coming up behind her. The sound of tires crunching over gravel had never sounded so good. Relieved, she turned to wave down the driver.

Instantly, her jubilation drooped.

It was Court.

CHAPTER FIVE

COURT BRAKED HIS truck to a stop behind Sabrina's old green '69 Chevy truck. Since the hood was up, he decided it was safe to assume that the problem was more than a lack of fuel. She stood, her hands braced against the left front fender, glaring at him. With her tight jeans, the T-shirt and length of brown hair streaked with gold and fashioned in some sort of half-bun, half-ponytail, she was far too welcome a sight for his comfort. With the next puff of sultry air, she swiped a wisp of hair back from her face, then turned toward him and planted both hands firmly on her hips in preparation for telling him to get lost, he suspected.

Court smiled, a gesture that relaxed across his mouth and took him by complete surprise. It wasn't her expression of annoyance that sent his lips curling upward, it was how much she reminded him of that little girl who used to follow him all over her daddy's ranch. Tall, almost lanky, but over the past couple of years she'd filled out in all the right places, he noticed with growing appreciation. Time and maturity had sculpted the once girlish and impish features of her face into that of a beautiful and seductive woman's. He suddenly remembered how he'd loved to tug on her ponytail all those years ago. She would get fighting mad when he teased her that way. Within minutes her irritation would be forgotten, though, and she'd trudge along behind him once more. And then he'd do it again just to watch the metamorphosis from starry-eyed back to ready-to-kick-his-butt.

God, only Brin could make him recall his youth with any fondness at all. Court pushed away the past and climbed out of his truck. He hadn't stopped to reminisce, she needed help with her truck. Despite the fact that his old heap was a couple of years newer than hers, the '71 Ford he drove looked a hell of a lot worse for wear. But it ran like a new one. Court hadn't cared how the truck looked, only that it got him where he needed to go, in a hurry if necessary. And he damned sure didn't want to get stranded on one of these long, deserted stretches of Montana road.

Like Sabrina had. He frowned at the idea of her being stuck out here all alone, especially at night. She'd have to be more careful about maintaining her vehicle. It could be hours or the next day, even, before anyone happened down this road.

Bracing himself for her fury, Court adjusted his hat and started in her direction. "What's the trouble?"

She heaved a mighty sigh. "Well, now, if I knew the answer to that I'd fix it and be on my way."

"Run out of gas?" he suggested, biting back a grin as he brushed past her.

"Hell, no." She followed him to the front of the vehicle. "It just sputtered for a minute or two and then died. But the gas tank's half full."

Court scanned the engine. The strong, unmistakable

scent of raw fuel mingled with the heat rising from it. He removed the wing nut and lifted the air filter and cover from the carburetor and set it aside. He checked the choke, which appeared to be working properly.

"Try starting her again."

Sabrina quickly scrambled into the cab and turned the ignition. It still wouldn't start. An excessive amount of gas pumped into the carburetor, flooding it, as he suspected it would.

"Okay. Hold on a minute," he called out to her. Court skirted the hood and leaned into her open window. "Got a hammer or wrench?"

Still eyeing him suspiciously, she reached down and fumbled beneath the seat. When she rose she handed him a pair of pliers. "Will this do?"

Court pulled off his hat and placed it on top of the cab for safekeeping. "It'll do fine. Give me a minute and you can try starting her up again."

She nodded, her gaze slightly less suspicious.

Maybe there was hope they could settle this thing between them, after all. That would definitely be a good thing. He didn't like this gap dividing them. He strode back to the front of the truck and tapped the carburetor housing a couple of times with the pliers in just the way his older brother had taught him too many years ago to count. The carburetor in Court's first truck had had a penchant for sticking. A couple of good taps and the float would unstick, allowing the choke to function properly once more.

"All right," he called out around the raised hood. "Give it another try."

Sabrina did as he told her, and this time the engine almost started. She looked to him for further instructions.

"That's got it." After replacing the carburetor cover, he slammed the hood shut and walked back to her door.

"Then why won't it start?" she demanded crossly.

"The float was sticking," he explained patiently. He knew she didn't want to spend one unnecessary moment with him, and that stung more than his ego. "Give it a minute for some of the extra fuel to dissipate and it'll start." He passed the pliers back to her.

"Thank you." She tossed the tool onto the floorboard on the passenger side. "I appreciate your help," she offered without meeting his gaze.

"You're welcome." He studied her profile, remembering every little curve and hollow, the satiny feel of her skin. She'd just graduated from high school when they made love that first time. He hadn't intended for it to happen, though he'd wanted her so badly he could taste her. At nineteen most guys didn't care how they got their sex, as long as they got it. But Court had cared. Sabrina was much more than just another score on his rutting card. She meant a great deal to him for reasons too complicated to explain. And he was very much aware that she hadn't ever been with anyone else. He hadn't wanted to take advantage of her feelings for him, or her innocence. He knew that she still had stars in her eyes where he was concerned. But in the end, neither one of them had been able to stop. He'd left Montana the next week.

He'd left Sabrina.

And she hadn't forgiven him, for that time or the last. He was a selfish jerk.

Court swallowed the regret that welled in his throat, threatened his ability to take a breath. He knew he'd hurt her, but, at the time, he just couldn't stay. He couldn't stay now. But he could try to make amends.

She sat like a statue behind the wheel, staring straight ahead. Several moments passed before Court realized that she didn't intend to say anything else.

He would have to take the first step. "What's the deal with the Double K?"

Her gaze shot to his at the question. "What do you mean?"

"Where are all the horses?" He replayed what he'd seen at her place and shrugged. "I didn't see any when I was there the other day."

Pain shattered the irritation in her eyes. "I have horses. You just didn't see them."

"And where were they then?"

Silence.

An uneasy feeling crept behind the defensive shield Court fully intended to hold in position between what his heart wanted to feel and what his head told him he should. "I don't mean to be unkind, Brin, but the place looked in pretty bad shape. The house needs painting. I noticed a lot of fencing that needs repairs. Who's taking care of the ranch for you now?"

The look of pain evaporated as fast as it had appeared, only to be replaced by another blaze of what looked like anger. "Not that it's any of your business, but I take care of the place myself."

His uneasiness sharpened. He rested his hands on the open window. "You don't have any hired help?"

"No." She resumed her vigil of watching the road directly in front of her.

Something Daniel Austin said that first day Court had seen Sabrina echoed in his ears. "Did you sell all the horses? Have things gotten that bad for you financially? Where's your mom? I thought she married again." He fired the barrage of questions at her, earning himself a heated glower.

"Is this thing ready to start now? I have to go."

Before she recognized his intent, Court jerked the door open, reached over the steering column and snatched the keys from the ignition. Shoving the keys into his pocket, he quickly drew back from the blast of outrage that lit her eyes.

"What the hell are you doing? Give me those keys!" she demanded furiously.

"No way." He backed off a step when she bounced out. "You're not running away from me again. We're going to talk, Brin, whether you like it or not."

"Court Brody, you give me those damned keys." She got right in his face, nose-to-nose. Her tall, lithe body vibrated with the anger he could see in those dark eyes. "Don't you dare accuse me of running away. You're the damned master at it."

He ignored that cutting remark. "As soon as we talk I'll give you the keys," he explained calmly.

"Fine. I'll walk." She flung the words at him like stones intended to shoo a pesky critter away, then started up the road in long, purposeful strides.

He settled into step next to her. "Fine. I'll walk with you. I don't have anything else to do this afternoon."

Sabrina admitted defeat, pivoted on her heel and strode back to her truck. When Court set his mind to something there was no changing it. She would just have to tolerate him until she could start her truck again. But he couldn't make her talk. Though she appreciated his help, she had nothing to say to him. Deciding to ignore his presence altogether, she leaned against the door and folded her arms over her chest. Let him talk until he was blue in the face, it wouldn't change anything.

She'd seen him take that man, Benson, away. Jed had called Benson a traitor. Court's actions could only mean that he had fallen completely under Neely's spell. Whatever happened to change Court, he wasn't the man she once knew. Nothing at all like the man she had…loved for most of her life.

He propped one hip against the truck right next to her. "Tell me what's going on with the ranch," he urged quietly, his tone so sincere she could almost believe he actually cared.

Sabrina closed her eyes. No, she reminded that foolish part of her that clung to any shred of hope, he doesn't really. He's just playing the hero right now. Aiding a damsel in distress. Pumping up his own ego. Nothing more.

Sabrina opened her eyes to his seemingly genuine gaze and tamped down the reaction that instantly gripped her by the heart. "My ranch is no longer your concern. *I* am no longer your concern." Not that she ever really was his concern. "Charlie and I are doing just fine on our own."

"So your mother isn't involved with the ranch anymore?" he persisted, undeterred by her declaration.

Sabrina released her impatience in a long, exasperated breath. "Mother lives in Florida with Norman, her new husband. Charlie and I share the running of the ranch."

Doubt flickered in that intent gray gaze. She knew he was recalling the sad state of the house and the barn. But she was doing the best she could. And he was right, there were fence repairs that needed to be made, as well. He didn't understand how difficult it was for her alone. Charlie was almost no help. But she had no intention of telling Court. Tears burned the backs of her eyes and Sabrina resisted the urge to cry. She would not humiliate herself further by crying on Court's shoulder, as tempting as that thought was.

"So you've sold off the horses to survive?"

His assessment hit the mark. Sabrina winced inwardly. There had been horses on the Double K for three generations. Now there were only two mares about to foal and a thousand things that needed to be done that she either didn't have the know-how to do herself or the money to pay someone else. Not to mention time. She glanced at the sun and realized how late it was. There was never enough time.

"I have to go, I have chores to do."

"Wait." He placed his hand over hers on the truck's door handle. He moved in closer, using the full body contact as leverage against her. "Brin, talk to me," he murmured softly.

He pulled her hand free and turned her palm up. Her pulse leapt at the feel of his thumb as it glided over her palm. But it wasn't a sexual caress, he was tracing the callused signs of the hard work she did every day to survive. She couldn't fully discern the ravaged expression on his face when his gaze met hers again. She only knew that there was no way to fake that kind of emotion.

"I swear I'll do whatever I can to help you, if you'll only let me."

A couple of tears escaped her tightly clenched lids. "Just leave me alone, Court."

His strong body moved closer still, pressing along the length of her. "Don't push me away, Brin."

Who was this man that he could say the very words she had longed to hear for half a lifetime, and yet she had seen with her own eyes the evil he was capable of?

"I have to…" She paused to steady her voice. "You're one of them."

The whisper of his sigh was warm on her cheek. Her heart quickened, making her want to lean into the shelter of his big, strong body. She needed someone so badly. Someone to help her keep being strong for Ryan and for Charlie. She wanted Court. But it couldn't be Court.

"Things aren't always what they seem, Brin. You have to trust me. I'm not like *them*. Not deep down."

Anger rushed through her, pushing away all those softer emotions. Sabrina did lean into him then, glaring up at him in accusation. "I saw you take that man, Benson, away."

"He was a traitor," Court said cautiously, his gaze now guarded. "He had to be dealt with. It was for the best."

"Yeah, right." She flattened her hands against his chest to push him away. "For whose best? I'd bet my last nickel it wasn't for his."

Court easily resisted her efforts to put some space

between them. He placed his hands against the truck on either side of her to ensure she didn't try to escape that way, either. "You'll have to trust me on that one, too."

She shook her head, disappointment and hurt spearing her. "I don't think so. You're just like the rest of them, all caught up in Neely's spell." The reality that this was her son's father multiplied the hurt a hundred-fold. "I don't know what happened to you, Court, but you're not the man I used to know."

Impatience or something on that order kindled in those silvery eyes. "You think I'm the devil himself because I'm in the militia." She could feel the tension of his rising agitation in his taut body. "You're a part of it, too! What makes you so damned righteous?"

He was angry now. Sabrina flattened against the truck in an effort to escape the building fury she saw in his eyes. "I'm helping the children, not Joshua Neely."

"Oh, so that's different, right?" He braced his hands at his waist. "You're not really there for the cause?"

"That's right." She trembled then at the feel of rock-hard muscles beneath her palms. He was so much stronger than she was, part of her wanted to be afraid, but the rest of her knew Court would never harm her physically. "I could care less about the cause."

"Doesn't that make you disloyal?" he pressed, his gaze so intent on hers that she felt uneasy in spite of her certainty that she was safe with him.

"I suppose it does." A little burst of courage shored up her crumbling bravado. "What are you going to do about it? Get rid of me like you did Benson?"

The awkward silence that followed was filled with

tension so thick that Sabrina could hardly draw air into her lungs. She wanted to run, but the feel of his powerful body kept her glued in place rather than pushed her away. She wanted to look away, but something in his gaze, over which she had absolutely no power, held hers there.

"Don't push your luck," he finally said, his words measured, his tone slightly threatening. "Just because I consider your lack of dedication harmless, doesn't mean anyone else at the compound will."

"I don't care what anyone there thinks," she retorted. "Least of all you." A new kind of fear chiseled away at her resolve to stay strong. He was right. Every day she went to the compound she risked a great deal of danger. How could she continue to take such chances knowing that Ryan needed her at home? But how could she give up on Charlie? "I do what I have to do."

He brushed his knuckles against her cheek and she flinched. Disappointment flickered in his eyes. "So do I," he relented quietly. "I know why you're there, Brin. You want to make sure Charlie's safe."

She blinked. He read her too easily.

His fingertips trailed along the line of her jaw, then down her throat, making her shiver. She resisted the need to cry out at his touch. She had wanted, needed him for so long. But she could not allow herself to believe in him again. It hurt too much when he left.

"I'll keep an eye on Charlie," he assured her, his voice soothing, his words making her wilt with relief. "I can't promise you that I'll know what he's doing every minute, but I'll do my best to keep him out of trouble."

But she couldn't depend on Court. He'd left her in the lurch one time too many. "I can take care of Charlie myself. I don't need anything from you."

"Look me in the eye and tell me that," he ordered.

She glared at him. "You can't tell me what to do."

A glimmer of a smile tilted one side of his mouth. "I knew you wouldn't be able to."

She was losing valuable time here. She had to pick up Ryan and get home to start the chores. "I have work to do."

"All right." He dropped his hands to his sides, effectively releasing her from the prison his body made around her. "I'll come along and help."

Anxiety tightened her chest. He couldn't go to the ranch again. It was too risky. He might see something he shouldn't, even if Ryan wasn't home.

She shook her head. "I can take care of the chores myself, Brody."

He reached over her head and snagged his hat. "Maybe you can, but I've never seen a rancher yet who couldn't benefit from an extra pair of hands. I've been known in the past to work pretty hard for my supper."

Outright panic slammed into Sabrina then. She couldn't leave Ryan for so long. And if Court came into the house, the chance of him seeing a toy or picture of Ryan increased far too much for comfort.

"I don't know why you're doing this," she argued. "But I don't need your help."

He pinned her with a look that dissolved any hope she had left of him relenting. "I won't take no for answer. We need to talk some more. I told you I intend to set things straight between us."

Sabrina's mind raced to cover the steps she would have to take to protect her secret. "All right," she agreed, finally surrendering since he left her no alternative. "I have to make one stop first, though. You go on to the ranch. You can feed the mares in the barn. I'll only be a minute." She turned quickly before he could see the lack of truth in her eyes, but he stayed her once more when she reached for the door handle.

"Where are you going?"

She tamped down the irritation that rose instantly at his question. There was no more time to argue. She had too much to do. But first, she had to check on Ryan and Mrs. Cartwright.

"I always…" Sabrina moistened her lips and told herself that this was not a complete lie. "I always check on Mrs. Cartwright to make sure she's doing okay. She doesn't have any family, you know."

Court nodded. "I remember her. I used to exercise Mr. Cartwright's horses for him after he broke his hip."

Sabrina nodded, glad to see her ruse working. "Remember, they didn't have any children of their own, so there's no one to check on her now that she's alone."

Court looked thoughtful a moment. "Would you like me to go with you?"

Sabrina's heart slammed against her sternum with a new burst of fear-inspired adrenaline. "No, no. It's late. I'll never get the chores done now. You go on to the Double K, and I'll be right there."

He pitched her keys to her. "See you in a few minutes, then."

She watched Court's long, confident strides as he

moved toward his truck. A shaky breath shuddered out of her. That was too close for comfort. She knew for sure there were no toys or baby things in the barn or yard. So, all would be well for the moment. But before she allowed him into her house, she had to check every room he might set foot in to be sure there was no sign of her son.

Sabrina opened her door and started to climb in, only then realizing that Court hadn't driven away. He was waiting to make sure her truck started. She turned the ignition, and blessedly, the engine cranked. Without looking back, she headed toward Mrs. Cartwright's. The sweet old lady wouldn't mind keeping Ryan a few hours longer, but Sabrina sure hated to miss that time with him. She loved her little boy more than anything else in the world.

And no matter what it cost her or Court, she intended to keep Ryan safe and happy.

COURT DRIED THE LAST POT and placed it on the counter. "It's hard to believe Charlie's grown up enough to drive around the ranch." He chuckled, the sound making Sabrina feel too warm inside. "I can remember sneaking a drive around one of the pastures in my father's old truck when I was Charlie's age."

"Well, I just wish Charlie hadn't parked the truck smack into the watering trough," she said, laughing a little herself at the remembered image. Though she certainly couldn't afford to have the repairs made, Charlie had been so excited about his first driving lesson. And his happiness had meant a great deal more to her than some dumb pipe he'd broken in the process of learning to park.

Court's amused expression fell into lines of worry. "I can't believe you've been hauling water for the horses all the way from the house."

This was where things got sticky. She didn't want Court to know just how bad things had been around here. Those protective, older-brother-type genes would just kick in and then she'd never be rid of him.

"Plumbers are expensive," she said as casually as she could. She bent and placed the pot he'd dried into its proper place in the cabinet next to the stove. "I was planning on skipping the pipe repairs awhile longer and buying enough water hoses to cover the distance, but I haven't had time to pick them up." She shrugged. "Besides, lugging the water isn't such a big deal. Charlie helps."

"When he's here," Court countered. He didn't want to make Sabrina angry, but she needed help. He planned to have a talk with her little brother about responsibility. A talk he obviously hadn't been given since his father died so long ago. The Double K was falling apart around Sabrina's slender shoulders. She couldn't do it alone, no matter how tough she was. The thought of those hard-earned calluses on her palms twisted like a knife in his gut. No woman should have to work that hard. It wasn't right.

She tunneled her fingers through her hair and sighed. She was tired. Court could see it in her eyes and her posture. Dammit, this whole picture just wasn't right. How could things have changed so for the worst in such a short time? He pushed away the guilt that wanted to rise. Too many years had passed since he'd really checked on Sabrina. The last time they were together, two years ago, they'd been at a hotel in Livingston and she hadn't done much talking. But he'd done plenty of talking and taking. He swallowed at the regret that stuck in the back of his throat.

"Charlie's a teenager," she defended, "and he's having a tough time with all that raging adolescent stuff."

Court tossed his dry towel onto the counter and focused his attention back on the here and now. "I know all about how it feels to be a teenage boy. I was one. Remember?"

Sabrina blinked, her expression startled. His body had reacted to those memories all evening. Was she suddenly remembering those shared moments, too? Her every word, every look, every touch made him recall another one just like it from back when they were young. All he had wanted to do was get away from this place, and somehow her laughter and enthusiasm had always made life bearable in the meantime. The vivid images of their first time making love slammed into his thoughts. His body grew instantly aroused at the sweet memories, but his chest ached at the hurt he had caused by allowing it to happen. Court knew from the look in Sabrina's eyes that she was remembering the good as well as the bad.

She squared her shoulders and banished the longing he recognized in her eyes. "Things have been tough around here and Charlie's been more than a little frustrated," she offered in explanation of her brother's behavior.

Court moved in on her then, trapping her against the sink. He didn't care what motivated Charlie. He only cared that she needed him, and Court would not turn his back on that need. He couldn't be here for her like he knew she had once wanted, but he could do this. "I want you to let me help you, Brin. I can afford to—"

"No." She held up her hands stop-sign fashion. "I appreciate what you did today repairing that water pipe, and helping me with the chores. But I won't accept your charity, Court Brody, so just forget it."

Irritation buzzed in his ears. Repairing the plastic pipe had been nothing. "But if you need money—"

"I don't need money."

She was lying.

"I'm not blind, Sabrina," he said firmly, his impatience pushing past the tolerance he'd promised himself he would show her. "Don't try to sugarcoat things for me. This is Court you're talking to. Hell, I know this ranch as well as you do. I know when things aren't right. And this—" he lowered his voice, the effort clearly a struggle "—isn't right."

"I know you mean well, but I would rather handle things on my own. I've been doing it for three years. Why change now?"

Regret kicked him in the gut again. "All I'm asking is that you let me help just a little," he insisted, his gaze searching her face, then her eyes, looking for the surrender he had once wrought so easily in her.

But not this time, apparently.

Sabrina shook her head. "No."

He cocked his head and leveled his most intimidating glare on her. "Why?" He raised one hand when she would have argued his high-handedness. "Just tell me why."

Sabrina rubbed her tired eyes with the fingers of both

hands, then rested her face in her palms for a moment. There was no point in beating around the bush. Court always got his way. He simply wouldn't stop until he did. But not this time. Not the way he wanted to, anyway. She folded her arms over her middle and looked straight at him. "Because I don't want to get close to you again, Court. I don't want to depend on you in any way. It hurt too much when you left the last time. I can't let you do that to me again."

He blinked twice. Sabrina couldn't say for sure what it was she saw in his eyes then. A mixture of pain and anger, and maybe even regret.

"I know I hurt you, and I regret that."

A tiny shock reverberated through her at his admission. He stared at the floor for a few seconds, and Sabrina's heart foolishly pounded with anticipation at what he would say next. At last he continued, "I know there's nothing I can do to change the past or to even make up for it. I can't tell you that I won't be leaving again soon, because I will."

Unbidden, tears welled in her eyes. She had known he wouldn't stay, but hearing it said aloud made it more real, somehow. Sabrina swiped fiercely at the one tear that managed to escape. Dammit, why did she have to cry? To show him all over again just how much power he held over her even now.

Court reached for her hand, his own shaking just a little. Or did she only imagine it?

"Brin, let me be here for you for just a little while. I want to help you," he urged, a plea in his voice…and something else. "No hidden agenda. I just want to help you."

Her gaze flew to his and Sabrina knew in an instant what she'd heard in his voice. Court's eyes were bright with his own emotions. He wasn't openly crying as she was, tears streaming down her cheeks, but inside he was weeping. She could hear it in his voice and see it deep in those smoky depths. He truly wanted to help her. Slowly, giving her ample time to draw away, he pulled her into his arms and held her. Just held her.

"I swear I won't hurt you this time," he murmured.

Desperation tore through her. He wanted to make things right between them…but she could never allow him close enough to do that. Court wanted a clear conscience when he left Montana the next time. Could she live with her own conscience if she simply allowed him to walk away without telling him the truth?

Did she have a choice?

Ryan's whole future depended on what Sabrina did right now. If Court discovered her secret he might just demand joint custody. What kind of life would that be for a child? She could not risk Ryan's happiness.

Not for hers…not even for Court's.

CHAPTER SIX

WHEN COURT STOPPED at the gate to the compound after leaving the Double K, the guard rushed to his window. "We've been waiting for you to get back," the man said breathlessly. "Joshua needs you. Report to your quarters, Brother Brody. I'll let Joshua know that you're back right away."

Adrenaline burned through Court's veins, sending him on instant alert. He nodded and drove through the open gate. Once he'd parked his truck he double-timed it down to the lieutenants' quarters, the pounding in his chest keeping time with his racing thoughts. Had he made a wrong move? Said the wrong thing to anyone? He didn't think so. Maybe one of the men here had seen him at the Watering Hole with Austin. But that alone wouldn't be proof of anything. And Austin had taken care of Benson. No one could be the wiser on that score.

Whatever the case, Court had no choice but to play the hand he'd been dealt and see where it took him. It wouldn't be the first time, nor the last, that his life had hung in the balance. It was part of the job.

The front side of the long barracks building had been designated as housing for the upper echelon. Each lieutenant had a private room. Court slowed as he approached the last door on the far end of the building, his door. He forced an expression of calm and slowed his breathing. Three men waited outside his door. One was Ferguson, the other two were local boys new to the training program.

"About time you came back," Ferguson growled. "I was beginning to think we'd have to send out a search party to look for you."

Court's wariness moved to a new level. Ferguson was just waiting for a chance to take him down. Court would have to be particularly careful where this man was concerned. But not tonight. If Court had been made, Ferguson would have greeted him with a loaded nine-millimeter rather than a mere sarcastic remark. Maybe Neely would even lend Ferguson his Ruger as he had Court.

"Can't a man spend a little time with a woman without someone looking for him?" Court asked as he removed his hat and plowed a hand through his hair.

The two guys with Ferguson laughed outright, but not Ferguson, who glared at Court. "Next time," he grated, "let me know where you can be located. Joshua doesn't like to be kept waiting."

Court nodded. "I'll remember that."

"See that you do. Let's go."

Ferguson glowered one last warning in Court's direction, then strode toward the training center, Court following. The other two men brought up the rear. Court decided the presence of the other two men was for a show of force. Ferguson liked to make a big splash at everything he did. But instinct warned Court to be constantly on his guard. There was still the off chance he had been made and Ferguson just didn't know it yet. But Court doubted that possibility.

Once inside the training center, the other two men were dismissed. Ferguson nodded toward the rear of the building. "I think you know where we're going."

Court followed Ferguson into the hole Raymond had first led him to just two days ago. A new kind of tension surged through Court then. Maybe he was about to find out exactly what Neely was up to. That would suit Court just fine. He didn't relish spending any more time than was absolutely necessary with the man or his followers. Though it was clear to Court that most of the folks involved with the Sons and Daughters of Montana were good people, they didn't have any inkling whatsoever of the kind of man they had elevated to such a powerful position. The ammo room he and Ferguson had just passed spoke volumes about the man and his intentions.

Joshua Neely was a dangerous man. The only things Court needed to find out were on what level and with whom he was involved. Court felt certain that the people he saw every day supporting Neely couldn't possibly have financed an operation this elaborate. This level of activity and financial support was backed by a powerful group way beyond anything in or around Livingston, Montana. Court knew that the Black Order preferred to encourage groups like Neely's. People far too uninformed to understand who was taking them by the hand, but dedicated enough to follow orders without question.

Neely and the rest of the lieutenants were waiting in the white room. Though he'd fully expected the starkness, still Court reacted to the absolute white with its contrasting black table in the middle just like the first time he'd been led through the door.

"Now that we are all here, take your places, brothers," Neely ordered. "We have much to discuss."

Though Neely didn't ask any questions, Court could feel his gaze on him as he took his chair. All eyes focused on Neely as he settled back into his thronelike chair.

"We have been blessed, my fine lieutenants," he began. "Our faithful waiting has come to an end."

Court stole a glance at Ferguson, who was smiling, his gaze fixed firmly on their leader. As far as Court could see without turning his head, the rest of the men wore the same contented expression. Maybe Sabrina had pegged it right when she talked about Neely's spell.

"In five days' time we will receive the final shipment of arms that will ready us to do battle for our cause," he thundered. "And may God have mercy on those who would stand in our way."

Cheers went up around the room. Court sat, stunned, by the words Neely had just uttered. Battle? Was he intending to lead these unsuspecting people into some sort of war against local law enforcement? Silence fell over the room again as Neely scanned the waiting faces before him. Court adopted the same look of barely restrained enthusiasm as his counterparts to pass Neely's scrutiny.

"We will collect our shipment from Mr. Fahey at dawn five days from now. He has graciously agreed to meet us near the Canadian border." Neely leaned forward, eager to share his next words. "Mr. Fahey will be providing not only the weapons we ordered, but more important, the precise explosives we require, as well."

A new round of exuberant cheers and shouts roared from the men, while a dead calm settled over Court. *Fahey.* He knew the name. The man was the most notorious arms dealer north of the Mexican border in the Bureau's files. If Fahey was involved, this was big. He didn't waste his time dealing with small fish. Court swallowed in an effort to wet his suddenly dry throat. He would find a way to get word to Austin, if not tonight, first thing in the morning.

Fahey was a serious threat. He dealt in many types of explosives, but he specialized in one particular very new, very experimental type…something easily concealed yet that carried a hell of a casualty rate with massive property damage.

Demo, short for Demolition, was designed for use in blowing up buildings, or whole city blocks. A small amount went a very long way, making it easy to conceal for delivery to the target. The explosive was incredibly expensive and few dealers handled it. Fahey was the number one source for Demo.

Court's gaze moved back to rest on Neely. The man's pleased smile at the unity and complete obedience before him made Court feel physically ill. He would stop this man…one way or another.

"Now, my faithful lieutenants, we must make plans," Neely announced, garnering another round of rowdy cheering.

As if sensing Court's disloyal thoughts, Neely turned in his direction. His smile widened as he placed his hand on Court's. Court resisted the urge to jerk it back; instead he manufactured a pleased expression.

Neely leaned toward him. "Brother Brody, it's very important that you remain close to the compound during the upcoming days. If some need requires that you leave for a short time, ensure that you leave word with Brother Green as to your whereabouts. Our time is close at hand. We must not be late for the calling."

Summoning his most humble and heartfelt tone, Court placed his free hand over Neely's and said, "It's an honor to serve you, Joshua. I'll be ready."

Neely nodded his approval. He squeezed Court's hand before releasing it. "With Mr. Fahey's provisions, we shall prove victorious."

Court joined the other men, who were still cheering and boasting of their dedication to the cause, but he didn't miss Ferguson's menacing glare. Court only smiled at him, adding insult to injury. The man was seriously worried about Court's relationship with Neely. Ferguson turned away and added his booming voice to the others.

The stakes had just been upped. And Ferguson would do whatever necessary to protect his position as Neely's right arm. Court would have to watch his back around Ferguson, but he had suspected that from the beginning.

Leaving again tonight would be too risky, Court decided. First thing tomorrow he had to find a way to get word to Austin about the delivery from Fahey. Court caught Ferguson's evil, assessing gaze on him again. But right now Court had to worry about surviving the night.

SABRINA SCANNED the training center once more for Court or Charlie. A group of men were dismantling and cleaning weapons in one large classroom on the first floor of the building, while others were listening to an instructor Sabrina didn't recognize describe the steps involved in grenade handling in another classroom. She shivered in spite of the sweat rolling down her back. It was hot as Hades outside, but the goings-on before her chilled her from the inside out.

She hurried past the doors, peeking through each as she passed. She paused at the weapons room. The sight of all those guns made her stomach roil.

"Looking for someone?"

Sabrina whipped around at the sound of the condescending male voice behind her. Thad Ferguson looked her up and down before settling his leering gaze back on her face. A rifle hung from a strap over his shoulder.

She resisted the almost overwhelming urge to back up a step. No way was she giving this overzealous soldier the satisfaction of knowing he'd scared the daylight out of her. "I was looking for Court Brody."

Something changed in Ferguson's expression, hardened, turned even meaner. "Well, he's not here."

Sabrina swiped her damp palms on her thighs. "Do you know where I can find him?"

"Maybe." His gaze traced the fit of her jeans once more. "What do you want him for? Maybe I can help you with whatever you need."

Sabrina tamped down the urge to shudder with revulsion. She had to think of some acceptable excuse for needing Court. "He…he started some work at my ranch for me last evening. I wanted to make sure he still intended to finish the job like he promised." There, she relaxed a bit. That sounded logical. Anxiety twisted inside her all the same, making her want to run. "It'll…it'll only take a minute for me to ask him."

Ferguson studied her a moment longer, weighing her words, she supposed. It was then that she noticed the slight puffiness of his left eye. She wondered if he'd been in a late-night brawl at the Watering Hole. Most of the jerks around here hung out there.

"Since Brody did a little something for you, what'd you do for him?" he asked with a vulgar grin.

Fury ignited her courage. "Are you going to tell me where he is or not?" she demanded. "I don't have all day."

"My, my, you're a feisty thing, now, aren't you?" He moved closer, but she held her ground. "You need a real man to calm you down, not a wuss like Brody. I'd be more than happy to show you the difference."

Feeling entirely too brave for her own good, Sabrina smiled at him. "Well, I'll tell you what, Ferguson. When you run into a real man, you tell him to give me a call."

His face reddened and he narrowed his gaze at her. "Don't get smart with me, woman, or I'll put you in your place. Hell, you might even find you like my tactics."

"Just tell me where to find Court." This conversation had taken a definite turn for the worse.

"I'll do you one better than that." He snagged her by the right arm. "I'll show you."

Sabrina jerked and tugged with all her might to free herself from the ape dragging her across the room, but his iron-clad grip wouldn't give.

"Turn me loose," she warned when he hesitated at the bottom of the stairs leading to the second floor.

He sneered at her. "You said you wanted Court. I'm only taking you to him."

With seemingly no effort at all, Ferguson forced her up the stairs. She would never have imagined the gorilla would be that strong. Her heart threatened to burst from her chest. The sting of tears blurred her vision. She had to fight him. He could have anything in mind. And none of the others would help her.

When they entered the upstairs hallway, Sabrina glanced both ways, looking for an avenue of escape. If she could free herself from this lunatic she would just have to take her chances with the stairs. That appeared to be the only exit.

She had to get away.

He shoved her through a set of double doors into a large room. She paused in her struggle with Ferguson and hesitantly surveyed the area. Training mats were scattered like throw rugs over the floor, effectively sectioning the room off into three separate areas. Pairs of men were doing what looked like martial arts training at each set of mats, while others observed their display.

Ferguson nodded to the group on the far side of the room. "He's over there."

Her gaze followed his gesture, but it wasn't until the observers shifted slightly that she got her first glimpse of Court. He and another man were going at it pretty hard. Sabrina flinched when one blow caught Court squarely on the left cheek. As Ferguson escorted her across the room it became quite clear, though, that Court had the upper hand. Sabrina released the breath she hadn't even realized she'd been holding until then. The thought of Court being hurt was almost more than she could bear.

Both men had shed their shirts. Sabrina's gaze riveted to the glorious sight of Court's sweat-dampened torso. Her fingers tingled with the memory of that amazing terrain. Rock-hard muscle flexed and bunched as he moved around the mat, throwing punches or avoiding those of his opponent. The two circled each other in a wary dance of sorts. Court's more gold than brown hair fell across his forehead in thick locks. His intent focus never left his opponent.

Sabrina's heart triple-timed into a quick tattoo that had nothing to do with fear and everything to do with Court Brody. Would her son be as confident and physically strong as his father? She hoped that would be the case. But she prayed with all of her heart that Ryan would not be cursed with Court's restless heart. She had to find out what had happened to turn him away from the job with the FBI that he seemed to love so. Could it be that he simply couldn't stay in one place or do one thing for too long without losing interest?

Sabrina frowned as she considered their surroundings. Court wasn't like these men, she was sure of it. He might appear so on the surface, but she knew that he was a good man beneath that promilitia exterior. Why else would he insist on helping her when she had made it clear that she didn't want his help?

Guilt...maybe. He wasn't a fool. He knew he had taken her comfort and then walked away without looking back. He could have at least called. But he hadn't. Sabrina reminded herself as she watched him throw the other man to the mat, that Court would leave this time, too. He'd said as much last night. She knew better than to count on him…or to fall in love with him again. She knew better than anyone that there was no future in loving Court Brody.

Her heart ached for what her son would never know. He would never experience the love of a father or share those moments that only a father could create. Sabrina blinked back the moisture building in her eyes. She had to keep her senses about her. She could take care of Ryan. She could give him everything he needed to make up for his lack of a father. The reminder that she'd spent so little time with him yesterday zinged her already battered conscience. She'd felt so guilty, in fact, that she had begged off her teaching duties for the next couple of days. The only reason she'd showed up at all was to check on Charlie, but she couldn't find him.

Once she'd spoken to Court and had his assurance that Charlie was okay, she would get back home to her son. With Court stopping by in the afternoons to work on repairs, that wouldn't leave her a lot of time with her baby. By the time she picked him up last night after Court had gone, Ryan was asleep. For the next couple of days her mornings were all she would have with him. As bad as she hated to admit it, she needed Court's help. She rationalized her acceptance by telling herself that he owed it to her…but the truth was she wanted to see firsthand what kind of man he really was. To disprove the doubts still lurking in those fearful corners of her mind. Just in case…

"Brody, got something here for you!" Ferguson shouted as Court prepared to deliver the final blow that would take the other man down.

Court looked up, his gaze connected with Sabrina's and his opponent struck. The other man delivered a stunning blow to his midsection, and then his upper back. The other man walked off the mat the winner, leaving Court struggling back to his feet.

Ferguson held her back when she would have run to him. "Let me go!" she demanded.

The bastard only grinned at her. "Be patient, he'll stagger over here soon enough."

Court shoved the hair back from his eyes and headed in their direction. He winced and one hand flattened against his abdomen. Sabrina ached to touch him, to ensure that he was indeed all right.

"Sorry, brother, looks like my timing was off," Ferguson offered by way of explanation for his actions.

Court stared at him hard, his face giving nothing of what he was thinking away. "No problem. I can take a loss now and again, same as you."

Ferguson's face turned that deep shade of red again. Sabrina wondered if that explained his swollen eye. He finally released his death grip on her arm.

"Maybe she can do something to make up for my untimely interruption." Ferguson glowered at Sabrina one last time before storming away.

Court nodded, indicating a job well done to his eager opponent, she supposed. Sabrina suddenly recognized the other man as Clydus Beecham. His wife was one of the teachers who helped with the children. Court turned back to her then, his gaze worried, searching hers for answers even before he spoke.

"What are you doing here, Brin?" He grabbed a towel from the stack on a nearby bench and scrubbed it over his face, then rubbed his neck.

She remembered to breathe. Standing this close with him only half dressed did strange things to her ability to draw in any air. "I needed to talk to you."

He picked up his shirt and hat and started toward the door. "Couldn't it wait until this afternoon? You haven't forgotten that I planned on working on the barn roof today, have you?" His concern seemed to escalate as he guided her, placing his hand at the small of her back.

She shook her head since speech suddenly eluded her at the simple touch of his hand. Once in the hallway, he surveyed both directions, then pulled her close. "Is something wrong?" His deep, husky voice rolled over her, making her feel things she knew she shouldn't feel.

"I... Charlie didn't come home again last night. I've been worried sick." *I ain't coming back.* Charlie's words ached through her. A line of worry creased her brow even now, making her head hurt.

Court slowly lifted his hand and traced that line with the pad of his thumb. His fingers splayed on her cheek so he could lift up her chin to look her directly in the eyes. "Go home, Brin. I'll check on Charlie and give you an update this afternoon. I don't want you hanging around here. It's too dangerous."

He kept telling her that, yet he was here...and Charlie was here. "What else can I do? I'm worried about my brother."

"I asked you to trust me. Is it that difficult?"

She looked away from those silvery eyes. Yes, she wanted to say, but couldn't bear the lengths she knew he would likely go to in order to convince her that she could trust him. Court rarely gave up when he set his mind to something.

"I guess it is," he breathed softly. "I've never given you any reason to trust me."

Her gaze flew to his. The hurt there tugged at her, made her want to deny the words he'd spoken. "Things are different now," she offered. Dammit, why was she rationalizing? She hadn't walked away from him. She had known this would happen. Just as soon as she let him anywhere near her she started believing in him again, blaming herself for everything wrong that happened between them.

"Promise me you'll go home," he again urged, the plea in his eyes genuine. "I'll make sure Charlie's okay."

She nodded, unable to argue with his reasoning. She needed to get back to Ryan, anyway. "You'll be over about three?" she asked, double-checking so she could take Ryan back to Mrs. Cartwright's in time.

"Three." He tugged at her ponytail. "Now, get out of here, before I do something I shouldn't."

There was no mistaking the glimmer of desire in his eyes then. Sabrina's breath stalled in her lungs. He couldn't possibly still feel it as strongly as she did, could he? Before she said or did something foolish herself, she hurried away. Until she disappeared down the stairs, she felt his gaze on her. Her heart thudded at the idea that he still wanted her.

She was hopeless.

IT DIDN'T TAKE COURT LONG to find Charlie. The kid was target practicing with the rest of the boys his age. Ferguson and Bradley were leading the exercise. Court waited patiently until the practice was over. Ferguson already had it in for Court, no point in antagonizing the man further. Court's gaze narrowed as he considered the way Ferguson had manhandled Sabrina. He didn't want that lowlife SOB touching her. But he wouldn't have to worry about that happening again, he intended to make sure she stayed away from the compound. All he had to do was keep Charlie out of trouble.

The kid whooped when he hit the bull's eye dead center. Court smiled. He remembered the first time he'd been that lucky. His father and older brothers had picked him up and thrown him into the air over and over again. Court stilled. Where had that memory come from? He forced the past away. He didn't like to dwell on it, or the memory of his father.

"Did you see that last shot, Court?" Charlie shouted as he bounded in Court's direction. "I hit that sucker dead center!"

Court inclined his head in acknowledgment. "I did. I have to admit it was pretty amazing. Who taught you to shoot like that, kid?"

Charlie stared at the ground and kicked at a pebble. "My big sister," he mumbled.

Court felt another smile overtake his lips. He'd suspected as much. Sabrina was a pretty good shot. "Man, I wish I had a sister who could shoot like that," he said wistfully.

Charlie's head shot up. "Really?" He roped in his enthusiasm three seconds later. "She's a big pain in the butt most of the time," he qualified. "But I guess she's okay for some things."

"I guess," Court agreed, thinking of the way it felt to hold Sabrina in his arms. To make love to her and know that he was the only man she'd ever wanted. She'd said those very words to him two years ago.

And he'd left.

Had she found someone else? Court blinked at the memory blitz.

"Is it true that in a few days something really big is gonna happen?" Charlie jumped into Court's disturbing reverie with both feet.

The arms deal. The word had gotten around, even to kids like Charlie. Court almost shook his head at the notion of a good kid like Charlie being involved with scum like Ferguson and Neely.

"Could be," he hedged. "Where'd you hear that?"

Charlie jerked his head toward Ferguson, who was still discussing results with some of the other boys. "Ferg told us. He said things are going to start happening around here ánd we have to be ready."

Court reined in the urge to walk over and pound Ferguson into the ground. "In that case, you should be sure you get home and get yourself a good night's sleep."

"Home?" Charlie scrunched up his face into an exaggerated frown. "Why should I go home? She don't care about me."

She only cares about Ryan. Charlie's words from before collided with Court's earlier thought like a crashing jetliner. "You mentioned someone named Ryan before," he began slowly. "Who's Ryan?"

Charlie's eyes went wide. He looked as nervous as a long-tailed cat in a room full of rocking chairs. "You'll…you'll have to ask Sabrina about him."

Jealousy stabbed deep into the center of Court's chest. She sure as hell hadn't said anything about another man last night. And Court sure didn't see any evidence of a man's touch around the Double K.

"I'll do that," he said, to put the kid at ease. "It's no big deal, I just wondered, that's all." Yeah, right. He was jealous of a man he didn't even know, over a woman who didn't even belong to him. He was here to do a job. He wasn't supposed to get personally involved with anyone related to the case. The image of Sabrina filled his head, arguing otherwise. He had to help her, he reasoned. He owed it to her.

Another man or not.

Damn, he was getting his focus all twisted around here. He had to get this thing with Sabrina under control.

"Charlie, come on over here, buddy, and let's go over your scores," Ferguson called out.

"All right!" Charlie dashed off without so much as a goodbye.

Another wave of jealousy washed over Court. He swore at his inability to control his emotions. Sabrina and Charlie weren't his concern. He'd do what he could to protect them, but he had to keep his priorities straight.

Nothing could get in the way of the mission.

Nothing.

CHAPTER SEVEN

SABRINA STOOD A few feet away and watched as Court finished the last of the fence-mending. Yesterday he had spent the afternoon nailing down the loose metal roofing on the barn. A recent storm had blown several sections loose, causing a couple of leaks. Now the roof looked as good as new, or at least as good as it had during the last ten years. Sabrina was immensely thankful to have that worry off her shoulders. There was no way she could have afforded to pay anyone to come out and do the work. Going through the winter with those leaks would definitely have been a hardship.

Today, Court had worked diligently since noon on the fencing. Now that dusk was nearing he worked even faster to finish before he lost the light. Offering him a glass of lemonade seemed awfully lame considering the amount of hard work he had accomplished in such a short time, but she didn't have any beer in the house.

She still couldn't be sure if it was simply his guilt that motivated his actions, but whatever it was she was grateful. And he had been the perfect gentleman. Other than the caring embrace the night before last, he hadn't tried to touch her. That's when she had decided his actions were mainly related to a guilty conscience.

At first she had told herself that he owed her his help. After all, he had left her behind to have his child alone. But he hadn't known the consequences she had faced...alone. At the time, she had chosen not to tell him. She'd been angry. She had rationalized her decision with two simple facts—one, he obviously hadn't loved her, and two, his life was in D.C. while hers was here. It would always be here. She didn't want his offer of marriage out of a misplaced sense of responsibility. She knew Court too well. He would have insisted upon marrying her and moving her and Ryan off to the city. Based on obligation, the marriage would never have lasted. She didn't want to raise her son in the city.

None of those facts had changed in the past two years. Court would never stay here. Whatever his fascination with the militia, he would grow bored with it and leave again. And he still didn't love her. But now there was another factor to consider, his reaction to what she had done. If he discovered her secret, what would he do? He might just be so angry that revenge would be his recourse. She would not risk him trying to take Ryan from her. Nor did she cotton to the idea of sharing her son, with him living so many months out of the year with his father far away from her. She just wouldn't take that chance. No matter what her traitorous body urged as she stood watching Court. Her pulse raced, sending her heart into an erratic rhythm. Warmth pooled in places that made her restless. And desire sang through her veins.

She knew the symptoms all too well. As a lovestruck teenager she had watched him countless times as he completed the chores around the ranch. Whether it was mending fences, feeding the horses or even mucking out stalls, she'd been mesmerized by his every move. Engrossed in his every word.

Now, more than a decade later, not much had changed in that respect. Despite her absolute best efforts, she was still spellbound by his effortless grace. No one moved like Court Brody. He had a unique body language that no other soul on earth could duplicate. So much muscle, yet so lean, his hard body would make any woman yearn to touch him…to smooth her palms over that rugged terrain. She swallowed. Those faded jeans hugged him like a second skin. Beltless and riding low on his hips, the worn denim allowed a breathtaking glimpse of his tan line. He'd taken his shirt off and slung it over the fence, revealing that amazing torso, which caused more skips in her already irregular heartbeat. His face was the finishing touch to a masterpiece, with lines and angles that chiseled his features into pure masculine beauty. His smoky eyes completed the stunning picture.

And when he smiled…Sabrina's breath caught at the memory of a true Court Brody charmer…it was a sight to see. Her son was a perfect replica of his father.

Forcing herself a step closer, the melting drink clutched in her hand, Sabrina moistened her lips and produced a bright smile. "Looks like you've about got it whipped," she said cheerfully.

He paused, removed his hat and wiped his brow with his forearm, then smiled. Sabrina melted on the spot. Her gaze slid down his awesome chest, following that line of sandy chest hair until it narrowed and plunged into those low-slung jeans. Pure, unadulterated lust zinged her.

"Just about." He nodded at the glass in her hand. "Is that for me?"

Heat rushed up her neck and across her cheeks. She'd been so busy gaping at him that she'd forgotten what she'd come out here for. "Yes." She thrust the glass in his direction. "I thought you might be thirsty."

Thought, hell. She knew he would be. But it had taken her hours to build up the courage to approach him. She didn't want to feel this near overpowering attraction for Court. No matter how hard she tried to resist, to push him away, she just could not evict him completely from her thoughts…or her senses.

She had been in love with Court for as long as she could remember. But did she love him still, or was this hot-and-bothered routine just leftover lust from the past? She had been angry with him for so long, it felt strange to feel anything else. Need, gratitude, fear. She pressed a hand to her throat and commanded her body to calm. She was confused right now. So much was going on with trying to hang on to the ranch, taking care of Charlie and being the best mother she could be to Ryan, Sabrina felt as if she were swimming upstream with her head barely above water. Every few feet something else tried to jerk her beneath the surface, attempting to force her to admit defeat.

After downing half the glass of lemonade, he studied her for a few awkward moments. "You look tired, Brin. You ready to tell me what's really going on around here? I've pretty much summed up the most likely scenario."

Sabrina stumbled back a step at his intense gaze and his words. She didn't want to answer any questions. How could she tell him that the medical costs related to the birth of his son, which were not covered by the insurance company, had taken the very last of her paltry savings? And weeks of recovery time had kept her out of commission. The recent decline in the breeding market for small operations like hers, combined with the forces of nature over the past few years, and she'd verged on losing everything. It was only Daniel Austin's kindness that had saved the ranch.

Summoning her waning resolve, she folded her arms over her chest and met that analyzing gaze. "If you've figured it out, why bother asking me?"

He finished off the lemonade and handed her the glass, then tugged off his leather work gloves. "There's no need to get riled, I'm only asking." He surveyed the land around them as the sun slowly slipped behind the distant mountains. "I know how much this place meant to your daddy and I hate to see it go down like this."

Rage bubbled inside her. "Do you think I enjoy it? But I can only do so much alone." She snapped her mouth shut. She hadn't meant to say that. She didn't want him to know how difficult things were for her.

That silvery gaze collided with hers once more. "Your friend Ryan doesn't help you out?" he asked, wariness and something else she couldn't quite identify in his tone.

Fear kicked at her heart. He thought Ryan was a boyfriend. "I've already told you that he's none of your business. I didn't ask you to do this, Court. Not that I don't appreciate it." She struggled to keep her tone even. "But don't think that makes me feel obliged to you in any way, because it doesn't. I know better than to depend on you for more than one day at a time."

He drew off his hat again and threaded his long fingers through his hair as if considering her words. Then, his eyes holding her in that same old trance, he took the three steps that separated them. When he'd moved in so close that she could feel the heat from his body, he lifted one hand to her face and pushed back a tendril of hair that had fallen loose from her ponytail. Her lips yearned for his. Dammit. She didn't want him to make her feel this way, but he did. She wanted him to kiss her…to love her the way she'd spent a lifetime loving him. She was totally, completely hopeless.

"I'll help you all that I can while I'm here." He lowered his hand, allowing it to drop back to his side. "And I'm not expecting anything in return. You and Charlie are like family to me." He let go a sigh of defeat. "A man's supposed to take care of his own. I can't promise you how long I'll be here, but while I am, I'll do whatever you'll let me to help. I've never been afraid of responsibility, Brin. That wasn't why I left. You know that."

So many emotions twisted inside her that she felt ready to run, run hard and fast. She knew why he'd left, all right. He didn't love her and he hated the life he'd had here. But he was right about one thing, he would never shirk his responsibilities. If he found out he had a son, Court would not walk away without him. What would he do if he discovered she had kept that son from him?

She didn't want to know. She only knew that she had

to put that distance back between them. Court Brody might be hanging out with Neely and his cohorts, but he was not like them. If nothing else, the last few days had proved what kind of man he was. Sabrina could not risk his finding out about Ryan. And she sure couldn't chance falling in love with him all over again. Her heart couldn't take the hurt when he walked away. And that was the one thing she could be absolutely certain of, he would leave. If he learned that he had a son, he would not simply walk away this time. He would likely want his son. That was a gamble she was not willing to take. This relationship had to stop here and now.

"How about I take you out to dinner," he offered with one of those killer smiles.

Sabrina bit back the cry of "yes" that raced to the tip of her tongue. She had to end it now. She had to go to that compound and drag her brother home. And she had to make sure Court stayed away from her and the ranch until that restless heart of his took him away just like before.

"You go on," she urged, praying he would do just that. She needed to pick up Ryan. "I appreciate what you've done, Court, but I don't want you to come back tomorrow."

Not giving him a chance to argue, Sabrina turned and rushed back toward the house. Allowing him this close was a mistake. One she wouldn't make again.

COURT SCANNED the quadrangle, squinting to see any movement in the darkness. He studied the guard in the observation tower next to the dining hall. The man turned like clockwork. Court waited patiently until the guard was in the twelve o'clock position again and

Court made his move. Wearing black jeans and T-shirt and his hat to shield his face, he should blend into the darkness well enough not to be seen, but there was no use taking chances.

Once he'd reached the far corner of the meeting hall, he waited, watching the guard in the tower directly behind the training center. Again, he waited until the man turned his back and Court felt fairly confident he had ninety seconds or so. He stole across the quadrangle to the training center, pausing before entering the door to listen for any sound. After several minutes of uninterrupted silence, Court slipped inside the building.

The classrooms that lined the left side of the first floor were dark, as was the large open area to the right where arms training was conducted. At the rear of the room, Court took the stairs going down rather than up. The only things upstairs were a couple more classrooms, a latrine and another large open area for hand-to-hand combat training.

Neely kept the communications center manned twenty-four hours a day. Court was certain his presence would not be considered unusual if he merely sat down at one of the open tables and reviewed intelligence. Any lieutenant was authorized that access. The fact that it was well after midnight might seem odd, but all he had to do was say he couldn't sleep. Court wanted to look at old data, to see if he could find any link to previous contact with the Black Order. This morning's status meeting had included a review of recent intelligence, which revealed nothing significant in Court's opinion.

He needed to pinpoint Neely's goal as soon as

possible. Before the arms deal went down would be nice, but highly unlikely. The sooner he got the information he needed, the sooner he would be out of here. Austin had gotten excited about the scheduled deal with Fahey. Whether Court could connect Neely to the Black Order or not, Austin intended to take the man down when the business with Fahey took place. Court had given Austin the time and place of the rendezvous. Austin would arrange the bust with the ATF. All Court had to do between now and then was stay alive…and, of course, dig up what he could.

At the bottom of the stairs Court paused to listen again. The basement was comprised of four rooms, each leading into the next. The place was as dark as a tomb. He shrugged off an uneasy feeling as he moved through the first room. Staying alive might be more difficult than usual. He was having trouble focusing on the mission, and that was highly unusual…and dangerous.

It was Sabrina, he knew. He couldn't bear the thought of her working so hard. The memory of the calluses on her hands tore at his heart. How would she ever survive with only two mares about to foal? It wasn't likely that she had enough money stashed away somewhere to tide her over until she built her herd up again. Hell, she obviously didn't even have the money for needed repairs. Court was going to have that long talk with Charlie when this was over. The kid had no right running off and leaving his sister without any help like that.

The irony of that thought struck Court so that he had to stop to catch his balance. Who the hell was he to give lessons in not running away? He couldn't wait to get away from this place when he was Charlie's age. But had Court done the right thing? He refused to consider that question. He had done the right thing. His life was with the Bureau. There was nothing here for him. Nothing that made him want to stay.

As if summoned to make a liar out of him, Sabrina's image filled his confused mind. He scrubbed a hand over his face and pushed the picture from his head. Sabrina was not his responsibility. Why was it that he couldn't ever put her completely out of his head? Not even when he buried himself in his work back in D.C. What was it about her that made him ache to hold her, gave him pause when he was certain he knew what he wanted?

Whatever it was, in a few days, a couple of weeks, tops, he would be out of here. He would protect her and Charlie as best he could, but he would not allow himself to become physically involved with her again. He'd hurt her once. He would not do it again. No way.

As Court neared the tunnel's secret door a sound to his right diverted his attention. Drawing the weapon tucked in his waistband, he moved silently in the direction of the sound. A solid thud alerted him that his prey did not know his way around the area in the dark. A hissed swear word gave away his follower's exact position. Three seconds later Court had the barrel of his Beretta pressed to the back of the man's head.

"Don't move," Court ordered quietly. "This way." He ushered his prisoner back toward the stairs. "Very carefully."

Court could hear the man breathing, fear rising inside

him. It surprised Court to find another traitor, or snooper, at the very least, among Neely's followers so soon. All the lieutenants knew their way around. They definitely wouldn't be sneaking around in the dark. Unless whoever it as had a hidden agenda like Court. At the bottom of the stairs, Court flipped a switch and a fluorescent light high above the stairwell blinked to life.

A long gold-and-brown ponytail hung down his prisoner's back. Court frowned. "Sabrina?"

She whirled to face him, the fear in her eyes immediately changing to anger. "You scared the hell out of me!" She looked ready to tear off his head and spit down his throat. "What are you doing down here?"

He lifted a skeptical brow. "The better question is, what are you doing down here? I could have shot you." He lowered the weapon still leveled on her chest.

Her eyes went wide as if she only just then noticed the gun in his hand. "Is that…the gun you used on Benson?" Her gaze connected with his, uncertainty and fury warring there.

Did she think he'd killed Benson? How could he explain that the guy was safely tucked away until this was over? He couldn't. Disgusted with himself for even considering the question, Court pushed the weapon into his waistband at the small of his back.

"Yes, it's my weapon. Do you realize that it's past lockdown?" he added, using all his effort not to explode with the rage building inside him. He shouldn't feel this way. "Do you know what they'll do to you if they catch you here now?"

She blinked, but couldn't hide the renewed fear in her

eyes. "Lockdown? I don't understand. I just wanted to find Charlie."

Court dragged a hand through his hair and rubbed his neck. "They lock the whole compound down at ten o'clock every night. No one except the lieutenants is supposed to be outside the barracks after that." He pinned her with his gaze. "You don't belong here, Brin. What's Charlie going to do when you wind up dead because you were snooping around here like this?"

Her tremble was visible. "I didn't know. I just thought it would be easier to find Charlie once all the training was over for the evening." She shook her head. "I didn't know." Tears threatened to brim over those long, thick lashes.

Court swore under his breath. What the hell was he going to do with her now?

"I'll just…" She backed up a step. "I should go home now."

Court snagged her by the arm before she could take another step. "You can't leave now. If you try to go through the gate they'll know you were here."

She moved her head from side to side. "I have to go." A new kind of fear welled in those wide brown eyes. "I need to…to go—"

He pressed his fingers to her trembling lips. "You can't go, Brin. You have to come with me. I'll keep you safe until morning. Then you can slip into the children's classroom and no one will be the wiser."

She wanted to argue, he could see it in her eyes, but her survival instinct kept her quiet. Court ushered her up the stairs, then paused to switch off the stairwell light. Once outside, he retraced his steps, each time watching the guards in the observation towers until it was safe to move closer to the barracks. Sabrina didn't resist. She remained glued to his side as they stole through the darkness.

Ferguson would love to catch Court in a compromising position like this. The bastard had followed Court to Sabrina's house yesterday. When Court had gotten out of his truck at the edge of her driveway, Ferguson had taken off in a roar of souped-up horsepower and a spray of dust and gravel. Court wouldn't put it past the low-life scumbag to try to use Sabrina and Charlie against him somehow. Court had to find a way to keep Sabrina away from this place—Charlie, too, if possible.

Court unlocked his door and followed Sabrina into the dark room. He closed and locked the door before turning on the small reading lamp on the table near the bed. After removing his weapon, he placed it beneath the pillow on his bed. Sabrina huddled in a corner, her arms wrapped around her middle.

He flared his palms and shrugged. "Home sweet home."

All signs of fear vanished from her expression. She charged up to him and planted her fists at her waist. "I cannot believe you," she snapped. "How could—"

He pressed his fingers to her lips once more. And once more fire shot straight to his loins. "Shh. We don't want to wake the whole place."

A withering glare was her only response.

"You don't have to worry." He gestured to the bed,

trying to calm her fury. "There's plenty of room for both of us. I'll stay on my side."

The glare intensified. "There is no way I'm spending the night with you, Court Brody. Been there, done that, remember? I'm out of here and you can't stop me."

She made a move toward the door and he manacled her wrists with his hands. He pulled her around to face him with ease despite her struggle. "Dammit, Brin, think. I took care of Benson personally. Do you want to risk Ferguson or Jed or even Raymond taking care of you? Being here after lockdown is breaking the rules. Neely won't let it go unpunished, you can bet on that."

She jerked against his hold. "Maybe they'll let you take care of me like you did Benson."

Court took a deep breath and counted to five as he released it. It didn't help. "I didn't hurt Benson," he said quietly. "He's safe until this is over."

She shook her head, clearly confused. "Until this is over? What are you doing back here? You swore when you left all those years ago that you weren't coming back. Then two years ago you blow into town long enough to bury your mama and take me to bed, and *poof* you disappear again. What's the attraction now, Brody, didn't you get what you wanted last time?"

Court restrained his own fury at her words. She had never fully understood what drove him. She didn't understand now. "You don't know me as well as you think you do, Brin," he returned tightly.

"You're right, I don't." She relaxed in his firm hold. "I don't know you at all. The Court Brody I knew would never have gotten involved with a man like Neely." She closed her eyes and struggled with the emotions he'd seen welling there. She took a breath, a sob almost, and opened her eyes to his once more. "You know, with Charlie I can kind of understand it. He's young, confused, and he needs a male role model in his life. But you—" she shook her head again "—there's no excuse for what you're doing. You're a grown man who should know better."

Her pain ached through him. He had hurt her so badly. Nothing he could say or do would ever make it up to her. "Brin, I can't explain why I'm here to you. But I swear I didn't mean to hurt you." His fingers slid down her wrists to entwine with her long slim ones. "I made a mistake. Coming back here and dealing with my mom's death, it rattled me. I wasn't thinking straight."

"I see." She tugged free of his touch and turned away from him. "That night was nothing but a mistake?"

He rubbed at his eyes. "You know I didn't mean it that way." He took her by the shoulders and forced her to look at him again. She moistened her trembling lips, the move tugging at his flimsy restraint. "You know I care about you. I always have. I just couldn't be what you needed me to be. I can't now."

"Don't flatter yourself, Court. What makes you even think I'd want you now?"

He closed in on her and took her face in his hands, peering deeply into her eyes. The eyes he had seen in his dreams far too many times. "Maybe it's the way you tremble when I touch you." He traced the line of her jaw, then lower, down the smooth column of her throat. "Or the way your eyes go wide when we're this close. I can feel it."

She fought to control the trembling his touch evoked within her, just as he'd said. "You're one of them," she accused, a quiver in her voice.

In that instant, with her looking so deeply into his eyes, and her heart on her sleeve, he couldn't lie to her. "I'm not one of them. I've never been one of them."

She blinked rapidly, but not before a single teardrop slid down her silky cheek. "Then why are you here, pretending to be like Neely and his men?"

"Because it's my job," he admitted. A rush of relief that made him weak-kneed followed the confession. "The Bureau sent me here to infiltrate Neely's organization and assess what he's up to."

Horror danced across her pretty face as she absorbed the implication of his words. "But it's too dangerous. If they find out you could be…" Her voice drifted off with the unspeakable thoughts forming inside her head.

"I know how to take care of myself," he assured her, pulling her closer. His arms went around her and he drew her into an embrace that both eased his conscience and wreaked havoc with his senses. "I couldn't tell you the real reason I was here. I shouldn't have told you now."

She pulled back far enough to look into his eyes. "I don't like this, Court. What if—"

He smiled. It was nice to have someone care if you lived or died. "Don't worry. I've done this before. 'Careful' is my middle name."

"What are we going to do?" She scrubbed at the dampness on her cheeks.

"I'll get you over to the children's classroom in the morning. All you have to do is act as if nothing happened. If anyone asks questions, I'll just tell them that you were with me all night."

"What about Charlie?" Worry swirled in those deep brown eyes. "I don't know what I'd do if anything happened to him."

Court ushered her toward the bed. "Don't worry, I'll take care of Charlie. Right now, you need to get some sleep."

She looked at the bed and then at him. "I don't think this is such a good idea, Court. I mean—"

"I know what you mean." He drew the covers back and gestured to the right side of the bed. "Don't worry. I'll stay on my side."

"But I can't stay," she argued again. "I have to get home."

"Sabrina—" he settled a gaze on hers that he hoped conveyed the gravity of the situation "—you cannot leave tonight."

Hesitantly, she sank onto the white sheets. "You're sure my being here won't get you into trouble?"

Court couldn't prevent the smile that tilted his lips. "Your being here is nothing I can't handle," he assured her with a great deal more confidence than he felt.

But he would do what he had to…even if it killed him.

One last look at Sabrina as she slid beneath the covers and he decided that dying might be a hell of a lot easier than lying in that bed next to her until dawn.

CHAPTER EIGHT

WHEN THE DIGITAL clock on his bedside table blinked from 4:59 to 5:00 a.m., Court knew he would not live through one more minute of Sabrina snuggled on top of him. He had been fully aroused since crawling into bed with her. But he'd decided he could handle it until she fell asleep and wriggled closer to him…and then she'd wrapped those long legs around his and he'd had to put his arms around her. That move had proved a big mistake and negated any possibility of sleep.

He eased an inch or so closer to the edge of the bed, in hopes of disengaging from her without completely embarrassing himself or her. With her face pressed against his chest and her arms around his neck, he doubted it would be possible to accomplish the task without waking her. The heat between her thighs burned him through the layers of denim separating them, and beckoned to him on a base level that nearly defied control. Her breasts were flattened against him, their tight peaks making him ache to taste her. He licked his lips in dizzying anticipation.

But he couldn't do that…not this time. She meant too much to him. He couldn't hurt her again. Court closed his eyes with that last thought. He would not analyze that insight. He was leaving soon, he wouldn't pretend otherwise. Slowly, he lifted her left arm and eased it toward her side. She moaned softly and burrowed her face more deeply into the crook of his neck. Court gritted his teeth until the overwhelming urge to roll her onto her back and take her right then and there receded to a more tolerable level.

He had to move, do something…now.

Sabrina hovered somewhere just the other side of waking. She felt warm and contented for the first time in too long to remember, her body relaxed and languid against the hard muscular one beneath her. Court, she thought dreamily. She hoped this dream wouldn't end, for in it she was with Court, in his bed. Beneath the disinterested facade she adopted each day, in his arms—in his bed—is right where she wanted to be. Her hips arched instinctively toward the thick ridge of exquisitely hard, male flesh pressing into her pelvis. Court was the one and only man she had ever made love with. She wanted to make love with him again. She sighed and snuggled closer. A sound rumbled from his chest and Sabrina's heavy lids slowly drifted open, the dream that had felt so very real fading to black.

The room was still dark. It was early, she decided. Where was she? She struggled to clear the last remnants of the erotic dream from her groggy mind. Where was Ryan? Memories of last night's midnight adventures zoomed into vivid focus in her mind. *You cannot leave tonight.* She'd spent the night with Court. In his bed. Every sense she possessed suddenly honed in on the aroused male body beneath her.

Oh, no.

Sabrina scrambled off him and to the end of the bed. She barely caught herself before she tumbled over the edge. The bedside lamp clicked on and Court pushed to a sitting position, his gaze searching hers. She blinked, adjusting her eyes to the light. His hair was tousled, his shirt wrinkled from her attempts to climb inside it, no doubt.

"Morning, Brin." His voice was thick and husky. The sound sent goose bumps tumbling across her skin.

The way she must look abruptly slipped into her consciousness. She shot off the bed and gave him her back while she straightened her clothes and finger-combed her hair. What had she been thinking? How could she have slept in his bed?

"You okay?"

He was right behind her. Sabrina stumbled away from him, stubbing her toe on a nearby chair in her haste. She hissed a curse and rubbed her sore toe with the heel of her other foot. He probably thought…what did he think? He'd awakened to find her sprawled all over him. Instantly a flush rose in her cheeks.

"Good morning," she offered with as much enthusiasm as she could considering her current state. She stole a glance at the cause of her flustered condition. He was watching her too closely, worry lines etched across his forehead. He thought something was wrong with her, that's what he thought. And he was right, she'd lost her mind.

"I'm fine," she retorted. She tried without success to ignore the liquid heat throbbing between her thighs, not to mention the absolute ache in her breasts and the fierce pounding of her heart. If you could call that fine, she was damned fine. Just mindless, that's all.

He closed the distance between them with slow, cautious steps as if he feared she might make a mad dash for the door. "Look, it's okay that you…well, about the way we woke up." He glanced at the bed. "Nothing happened." He swallowed, the strain evident in the movement of muscle beneath tanned skin. "So, it's okay, Brin."

But it wasn't okay. It wouldn't ever be okay. Sabrina cried. She wasn't exactly sure if it was her own fear and frustration or his sweet sincerity, but tears leaked past her crumbling restraint and slipped down her cheeks. Her whole life was a complete mess. She'd almost lost the ranch. Charlie wanted nothing to do with her. And here stood the only man she had ever wanted, and she couldn't have him. The father of her child. Her baby. Oh, God. A sob tore from her throat and she quickly covered her mouth to stop the next one. She'd never in his life spent an entire night away from her baby.

"Aw, hell, Brin. Dammit, don't cry."

Court pulled her into his arms. She wanted to resist, but she couldn't. She just couldn't. He felt so strong. She needed someone to be strong for her right now, even if it was only for a little while.

"Please don't cry," he murmured next to her ear. "I never could stand to see you cry."

Her arms went around his neck and she held on with all her might. "I'm sorry," she said between sobs. "I can't seem to stop." She didn't have anyone in this world to hang on to except her son, and he was just a little baby. God, how she wanted to hang on to Court now—to someone strong enough to hold up the world pressing down on her shoulders,

He kissed her forehead. "It's okay. Cry if you want to." He held her tighter. "It's okay, Brin."

His lips grazed her cheek and her heart stilled in her chest. He didn't move, his mouth only centimeters from hers, his body rigid. Longing surged through her, pushing away the last of her inhibitions. She lifted her chin slightly, just enough to align their mouths. His breath was warm on her tear-dampened skin.

"I want you to kiss me," she murmured. She could feel his yearning almost as strongly as she felt her own. It crackled between their nearly touching mouths.

He licked his lips and she had to close her eyes with the wave of desire that washed over her. "Please," she whispered, anguish, fear, anticipation all clawing at her.

"Are you sure that's what you want?" He cradled her face in his hands and forced her gaze to meet his.

She nodded, then she tasted his full, wide lips. She closed her eyes as he took control of the kiss. She knew better than to let this happen. She knew her heart would pay the price. Court would be leaving soon, and she would be left behind once more.

But she could have him now, and, for once in her life, that was all that mattered.

This moment…this man.

His fingers moved deftly down the front of her blouse, slipping the buttons loose. He pushed the shirt off her shoulders, dragged it down her arms. His mouth closed instantly over one bare breast. He groaned with pleasure at the taste of her. She threaded her fingers into his silky hair and held him closer, urging him on.

When he had laved that breast to his satisfaction, he moved to the other, dropping to his knees. His hands splayed over her bare skin and slid down to the waist-band of her jeans. His mouth drawing long and hard on her breast, his hands opened, then slipped inside her jeans and panties, pushing them over and down her hips. Her legs trembling, she stepped out of the final barrier of clothing. She cried out when his mouth fell upon her mound. Deep inside, her feminine muscles constricted with the same need racing through her veins.

His heart threatening to burst from his chest, Court eased Sabrina back into the armchair behind her. He lifted first one leg, then the other onto his shoulders, exposing the pleasure place he sought. Thirsty for all of her, he lowered his mouth to that sweet, sensitive flesh. Her spine arched as she threw her head back in ecstasy, her fingers gripping the wooden arms of the chair. Desire burned inside him, hot and fierce. He wanted to bury himself deep inside this heat, but first he would pleasure her until she was weak from it. He traced a path with his tongue, delving into each honeyed recess, finding that special place that made her moan and whimper his name. He teased with his teeth, then sucked and licked until she squirmed for more. And then he gave her more. His arousal weighed so heavy with need for her that he wasn't sure he would survive the foreplay.

He thrust his tongue into that steamy, hot place, his hands kneading the satiny skin of her thighs. She screamed, muffling the sound behind her fist. Over and over he tortured her in this way until the spasms throbbed inside her, her release so violent it even rocked him to the core.

He stood, his gaze still feasting on her naked beauty, and slowly unbuttoned his shirt. She lounged in the chair, too sated to do anything but watch his methodical movements. Her legs were still spread wide apart, but her feet were on the floor now. Her small, firm breasts gleamed, the nipples thick and taut. He pulled the shirt from his jeans and dropped it onto the floor. Her gaze tracked his every move, her fingers still tightly clenched around the polished wood. He unbuttoned his jeans, then lowered the zipper, the sound echoing in the room. Her eyes went wide with anticipation as he lowered his jeans and briefs, then kicked them off.

She moistened her lips as she surveyed him from his bare feet to his disheveled hair. He eased back onto the bed, his gaze never leaving hers. She stood, moving slowly, like some ethereal vision, toward him, then she crawled onto the bed and over him. Her hair glided along his skin, making him tingle with renewed excitement. His arousal throbbed insistently, aching for release. He couldn't hold out much longer, but she would have to do the taking. He would not. Not this time. He would only offer her the pleasure she wanted. She kissed his chest, licked one nipple. Court fisted his hands in the tangled sheets beneath him, a sting of desire rushing through him all the way to his tip. Her damp heat grazed his arousal, his hips instinctively arched. She gasped, and he growled savagely. He needed to be inside her.

She smiled just a little, as if sensing his desperation. With one hand she reached between them and encircled him with her cool fingers. He shuddered. Watching him intently, she guided him to her entrance. Slowly, one hot, hard inch at a time, she sheathed him until her thighs flattened against his hips. Court shook with the mind-blowing sensations that washed over him as she sealed their bodies.

She was incredibly tight and so hot it took all his powers of concentration not to come right then. She made a sound, not quite cry, not quite moan as she began to rock back and forth, squeezing him to the point of pain. He watched as she moved, hesitantly at first, then more confidently, faster. Her long silky hair hung around her shoulders, concealing the breasts he wanted to see. He reached for her, took one taut mound in each hand. She arched instinctively toward his touch, her nipples stone hard against his palms.

She rocked faster, harder, her eyes closed in fierce concentration. He couldn't take his eyes off her. She was so beautiful. He kneaded those perfect little breasts, aching to draw one into his mouth, but she felt so good astride his hips he couldn't bear the thought of her stopping or even slowing down to fulfill that need. She gasped with the first wave of climax, her slick, hot walls tightened around him, squeezed, released, squeezed.

No more!

Court pulled her down against him. He kissed her hard and deep, then rolled her onto her back and thrust deeply inside her. She moaned into his mouth. He sucked her tongue inside him, then pounded out the desire burgeoning in his loins. One more to-the-hilt thrust and he poured into her. His fingers tangled in her hair, pulling her mouth more firmly against his. He flexed his hips again, sealing their bodies as one until the last remnants of pleasure faded.

He drew back far enough to look into her eyes…to see if she felt it, too.

Completion…not only the physical kind, but something beyond that…way beyond that. She smiled and gently caressed his jaw. This was why he could never, ever put Sabrina fully out of his mind. She was the other half of him.

SABRINA SAT IN THE MIDDLE of Mrs. Cartwright's living room floor and played with her son. Her heart thumped hard each time she looked into her baby's eyes. He looked so much like his daddy. Her heart fluttered at the thought of Court. Her face flushed even now at the memory of his bold, intimate loving of her body.

"What are you going to do, Sabrina? Do you think it's right to keep the truth from Court?"

She lifted her gaze to meet her elderly friend's. This was the first time she had ever told anyone other than the doctor who Ryan's father was. But she'd had to explain her actions somehow. Sabrina never stayed out all night, but she had warned Mrs. Cartwright that she might have to in order to find Charlie. For that matter, she never even dated. Mrs. Cartwright suspected something wasn't right, and there was nothing to do but tell her the truth.

Sabrina pressed a kiss to her sweet baby's head. "I honestly don't know. I've kept this to myself so long, it scares me to even say it out loud." She smiled down at her gurgling little boy. He was teething, and therefore, chewing on everything in sight. "What if I tell him and it's a mistake? The fact I'm still in love with him doesn't mean anything. I don't know that he ever really loved me."

Mrs. Cartwright frowned, considering, as she rocked back and forth in her ancient rocker. "But he's a good man?"

A smiled lifted the corners of Sabrina's mouth. "A very good man. I was a little worried there for a while when I couldn't figure out what the deal was between him and Neely, but I know now."

"He doesn't want to stay here?"

Sabrina sighed. "No. Court hates it here. Life was tough for him growing up. His father was a heavy drinker, and that took its toll, financially and otherwise, on all of them. Court couldn't wait to get away. I think he was born restless. I can't ever remember a time when he wasn't talking about leaving."

For a moment Mrs. Cartwright remained silent. "And you don't want to leave?"

"This is my home. How can I just up and leave? I have Charlie to consider. My father worked hard to keep the Double K going, just like his father before him. How can I be the one to let it go?"

"But you said you loved Court," Mrs. Cartwright countered.

She closed her eyes and tried to sort her tangled emotions. "I do love him," she admitted. She opened her eyes and rested her gaze on her dear friend. "I've always loved him, I just don't know if I can hold on to him."

The older woman shook her head slowly from side to side, her eyes taking on a faraway look. "You can't hold him, child, unless he wants to be held. Nothing, not you nor Ryan, will keep him here for long if he doesn't want to stay."

"I know." Sabrina pressed her lips back to her baby's soft hair. "I know."

"So what are you going to do?"

Feeling helpless, Sabrina lifted one shoulder and let it fall. "That I don't know." Her thoughts turned back to her brother. "I'll probably bring Ryan to you tonight and try to contact Court if I haven't heard from him about Charlie."

"You're not going back to the compound?"

Sabrina massaged the ache in her forehead. "It's the only thing I know to do. Charlie's my responsibility. I won't go inside. I can ask for Court at the gate." She dredged up a smile for the older woman. "I'll wait until Ryan is asleep and bring him over. You just keep my baby safe for me."

Sabrina considered Mrs. Cartwright's words as she drove Ryan home. She was right. Trying to hold on to Court would never work, Sabrina had known that years ago when he left the first time. She certainly wouldn't use Ryan to try to trap him now. If Court loved her, and wanted to stay, he would simply have to be the one to make that decision. In the meantime, she would keep her closely guarded secret. When, and if, he ever told her that he loved her, then she would tell him. And pray that he wouldn't grow to hate her for keeping his son from him for the past two years.

Then Sabrina thought of the look in Mrs. Cartwright's eyes when she spoke of not being able to hold someone. Could she have been thinking of some lost love in her past? Or now? That notion gave Sabrina pause. Mrs. Cartwright had been alone for nearly ten years now…and she was past seventy years old. But who knew? Sabrina shrugged. Maybe her friend had a secret, too.

A frown lined her brow as Sabrina started down her long drive. An unfamiliar vehicle was parked near her house. Anxiety tightened her chest. It wasn't Court. She glanced at Ryan, who was asleep in his car seat. She would just leave him in the truck until she determined who her company was. With the windows down this early in the morning, he would be fine for a few minutes. The temperature was still pretty cool.

Sabrina climbed out of her truck and closed the door quietly so as not to wake her baby. The man on her porch turned to face her just as she started toward the steps.

Thad Ferguson.

What could he want? "Morning," she offered in the strongest voice she could marshal. Fear niggled at her, but she ignored it.

He glanced at the sky, then settled that leering gaze back on her. "Yeah, it's morning, all right."

She swallowed, uncertain what he meant by that remark. "If you're looking for Charlie he's not here." She prayed nothing had happened to her brother.

He shrugged. "I'm not looking for Charlie." He glanced at her truck. Sabrina's heart surged into her throat. "I just thought I'd see how you were feeling this morning."

"I'm fine." Her voice sounded empty, hollow. That

little niggling of fear mushroomed and froze her to the spot at the bottom of her porch steps. "Why would you be concerned?"

He took one step down. "Well, I saw you come out of Court's quarters real early this morning and I just wondered if you'd gotten any sleep last night."

"Court and I are old friends." Her heart pounded so hard in her chest she felt certain Ferguson could hear it.

He grinned, a sleazy, hate-filled expression. "I'm sure you are. I wouldn't mind having you for a *friend* myself."

Disgust made her shudder inwardly. "If you'd get to the point, Mr. Ferguson, I'd appreciate it. I have chores to do."

He took another step down, closing in on her. "I just wanted to warn you about that friend of yours."

A new kind of fear rushed through her then. "He'd better watch his step," Ferguson warned, "and if you're smart you'll stay away from him. I've got a feeling Brother Brody isn't what he seems to be. And I've made it my mission in life to find out just what he's up to."

"I don't know what you're talking about." Her voice quaked, but she couldn't help it. She glanced around the yard for some sort of weapon to use on him, but found nothing. Court had pleaded with her to stay away from the compound and any of the militia members. She hadn't expected to find one on her doorstep.

"Maybe you do, and maybe you don't." He took the final step down, putting himself at eye level with her now. "But I'll be watching both of you. One wrong move and you'll be dead. You understand that?"

Dead. Oh, God.

Sabrina nodded, unable to speak.

"You tell your boyfriend that I'm watching him, too."

Ferguson strode to his big, four-wheel-drive truck and climbed up behind the wheel. Sabrina didn't move a muscle until he'd disappeared out of sight around the bend in the road.

She hurried to retrieve her son. She had to find a way to warn Court. Her fingers slowed in their task of releasing the car seat restraints, but she wasn't supposed to go back inside the compound. He had made her promise that she wouldn't. He'd already mentioned that he didn't trust Ferguson. Sabrina took a deep, calming breath. Court knew how to handle himself. She had to trust that.

But would he ever trust her again when he discovered her secret? Her gaze moved back to her son. She'd done what she thought was right at the time. What if she'd made a mistake? The mistake of a lifetime.

And what about Charlie? Could she just pretend it didn't matter when he didn't come home?

Or would that be another mistake?

COURT CHECKED THE TRAINING center once more that evening, but with no luck. Charlie was nowhere to be found. Damn. He'd promised Sabrina he would take care of the kid and now he couldn't find him. He'd try the firing range one more time. Maybe they'd been out on maneuvers and decided to do a little target practice before calling it a night. It wasn't dark just yet. Kids Charlie's age couldn't get enough of that stuff.

Sabrina slipped into his thoughts as he strode toward the back gate of the compound. He'd kept thoughts of her at bay most of the day, but it was getting tougher and tougher. He'd ushered her away this morning before he could change his mind and take her back to bed. There was no denying the emotions he'd felt this morning. He cared a great deal more for Sabrina than he'd wanted to admit.

Once this mission was over, the two of them would have to work this out. Court couldn't think past the moment right now, he had to stay focused. Distraction could get him killed. And Sabrina was definitely a major distraction. He hardened at the mere thought of her. She was the only woman who'd ever made him feel this way. The only one who'd even come close.

She deserved better than what she'd gotten from him. This time would be different. They would talk, make some sort of plans. His emotions were still too mixed up for him to fully comprehend what was happening between them. He only knew that he would do right by her this time.

Charlie's exuberant voice echoed in the distance, followed by two or three other adolescent male voices. Court hastened his step. The sooner he got the kid out of here, the better off they'd both be.

"Yo, Charlie," Court called out to the kid.

Charlie dropped out of the line of teenagers headed toward the dining hall and jogged over to where Court waited.

"Did you hear about my new badge?"

Court produced a smile. "A new badge?"

Charlie nodded. "Best marksman."

"That's great." Court chucked him on the shoulder. "Charlie."

The sound of Ferguson's voice made Court's skin crawl. The man stopped next to Charlie. "Don't forget about tonight," he reminded.

"Don't worry, I won't," Charlie assured him with renewed enthusiasm.

Ferguson shot Court a menacing glare. "I got plans for the boy," he said mysteriously before turning to stalk away. "Big plans."

Court had a bad feeling about Ferguson's plans. The man would do anything to get at him, Court was convinced of that. "What's up tonight, buddy?"

The kid's eyes sparkled with excitement. "Ferg's going to take me and a couple other boys who did really good today out for night maneuvers. He even said that he had something really special planned for me. But I'm not supposed to tell anybody."

Court's blood ran cold at the thought of Charlie out in the woods in the middle of the night with Ferguson. He couldn't risk that tonight's little foray was an innocent training exercise. Ferguson was capable of anything.

"That sounds great." Court glanced across the quadrangle at his truck in the parking area near the gate. "Can you do me a favor, Charlie?"

"Sure, name it."

"Can you come with me to get some stuff out of my truck?"

Charlie nodded vigorously.

Court led the way to his truck. Once at the door he opened it and reached beneath his seat for his weapon. "Get in the truck, Charlie."

"What?" The kid frowned, clearly bewildered at

Court's sudden change in tone, not to mention the gun in his hand, though it was pointed at the ground.

"Get in the truck and keep your mouth shut. If you make so much as a peep, you'll regret it."

The kid's eyes rounded in disbelief. He opened his mouth to argue but quickly snapped it shut. Court climbed in behind him. He started the vehicle and backed out. As he eased toward the gate he leveled his gaze on Charlie's. "Not one word. You got it?"

Charlie, shaking like a leaf, only nodded.

Court waited at the gate for the guard to open it. From the corner of his eye he saw Ferguson talking to another man. Damn. He needed to get out of here before that SOB saw him. The gate opened and the old truck lurched forward, at the same instant Ferguson looked their way.

Court didn't wait to see if Ferguson was going to question his leaving, he just got the hell out of there. He had driven several miles before Charlie worked up the courage to ask questions.

"Where are we going?"

"I'm taking you home," Court said bluntly.

Fire flashed in the kid's Korbett brown eyes—eyes that looked exactly like Sabrina's. "I don't want to go home."

"Well, I'm afraid that you don't have any choice in the matter." He shot Charlie an irate glare that had him slumping in his seat. "You see, kid, I'm trying to save your life. I promised your sister I'd take care of you, so don't give me any grief. You'll do exactly what I tell you."

"I hate my sister," Charlie mumbled, his voice trembling.

"That may be, but she loves you, and whether you deserve it or not, she wants to keep you safe."

"Ferg and the others are my friends. They'll keep me safe."

"No, Charlie, they're not your friends. Ferguson was going to take you out tonight and most likely do something really bad to you."

Charlie's face puckered as if he might cry. "I don't believe you."

Court shrugged. "You'd better believe me, because it's true. You think I would have risked trouble with Ferguson if I hadn't known you could be in danger?"

The kid thought about that for a moment. To Court's relief, it seemed to sink in through that thick adolescent skull of his.

"If you give your sister one more minute of trouble and I find out about it, I'll be settling with you," Court warned in no uncertain terms.

Charlie swiped at his eyes. "I don't wanna talk no more."

When Court parked the truck in front of Sabrina's house and shut off the engine, he turned back to Charlie. "You remember what I said, if you make one false move, I'll be the one squaring it with you."

"Whatever." Charlie jerked his door open and jumped out.

Court did the same, then followed him up onto the porch. He wouldn't be able to stay long. If he had any sense he'd get in his truck right now and get the hell out of here. But he had to see her. Had to make sure she was safe.

Charlie stamped across the porch, grabbed the key

from its hiding place behind a Welcome sign and opened the door without even knocking.

Court stepped inside after him and quickly closed the door in case Ferguson had decided to tail them.

"Charlie. Court!"

Court looked up at the strange sound in Sabrina's voice. She was sitting in the rocking chair that had belonged to her grandmother, a baby in her arms.

CHAPTER NINE

"I DIDN'T WANT to come back here," Charlie was shouting at his sister.

Court's gaze was riveted to the infant…no, not infant…bigger…toddler in Sabrina's arms. Why didn't she tell him she had a child?

"Charlie, please don't shout," Sabrina pleaded, her voice too controlled. "Just tell me what happened." She cuddled the squirming baby to her chest.

"He—" the kid stabbed an accusatory finger in Court's direction "—forced me to come back." Charlie's face was beet red and tears were shining in his eyes.

Court looked from Charlie to Sabrina, then to the baby. "I don't understand. You didn't tell me about…" He gestured vaguely, aware that he sounded…stunned.

"That's Ryan," Charlie explained. "He's *all* she cares about."

Court shook his head and frowned. This was Ryan? Then why the secrecy? He'd asked her about Ryan twice and she had avoided the question. No—she'd told him it was none of his business. Something very much like relief moved through him.

Sabrina glanced at Court with a wild, cornered-animal look before turning her full attention back to

Charlie. "Charlie, please, you don't realize how dangerous Joshua Neely is. You can't go back there."

"The hell I can't." He glowered at Court. "Just as
soon as *your* friend here leaves, I'm out of here."

Court accepted his new standing in Charlie's opinion.
He no longer considered Court his friend. Court was the
enemy now. The kid sure as hell had a short memory. But
Court had too many other things to worry about at the
moment to waste any energy on Charlie's tantrum. Like
getting back before Ferguson came looking for him.

Sabrina had a baby. The realization made Court feel
strangely disconnected. Why hadn't she told him? She
hadn't mentioned getting married, either.

"Watch me," Charlie was threatening. "You can't
make me stay."

The baby started to fret. Sabrina looked ready to
break down into tears. Frustration and impatience
erupted like a nuclear blast inside Court.

"Do you want to live, Charlie?" he demanded in his
most lethal tone. The kid just glared at him. "Because your
buddy Ferguson was probably planning on offing you
tonight. You were most likely going to have a little training
accident. I've told you that already. And obviously—" he
glared at Charlie for emphasis "—you've forgotten our
little discussion already. Ferguson cannot be trusted."

Sabrina gasped, her eyes round with fear. The baby
still squirmed as if disgusted with the situation, as well.

"You're…you're lying," Charlie stammered. "You're
the one I can't trust."

Court shook his head. "No, I'm not lying and deep
down you know it, too. Why would I lie to you?"

The kid swallowed, hard. "Ferg likes me."

"He doesn't like anybody," Court countered. "He was only paying special attention to you to win your trust. That's what men like him do. He would hurt you to get back at me."

"I still don't believe you," the kid shot back belligerently.

"You'll see soon enough," Court assured him. "Neely and his followers are going down, Charlie, and if you go back there, you'll go down, too."

"What are you, some kind of cop?"

"You have two choices," Court continued, ignoring his question. "You can either stay with your sister and behave yourself, or you can go into protective custody until this is over. What's it going to be?"

Charlie turned his angry stare on Sabrina. "I can't believe you're gonna let him do this to me."

"Charlie, it's the only way to keep you safe," she tried to explain. "Court is trying—"

"Don't even talk to me," he shouted. "All you care about is that bastard kid of yours, anyway."

Sabrina visibly faltered. Tears rolled down her cheeks and her lips trembled. She reached out to him. "Charlie, I—"

"Stay away from me." He batted her hand away.

Rage exploded in Court's veins. He grabbed the kid by his shirt collar and yanked him close. "One more word out of you, and I swear to God, I'm going to kick your skinny butt." Charlie's face went white, his eyes rounded. "You will not speak to your sister like that, do you understand me?" Court barely restrained the urge to slap him silly.

Charlie was nodding his head so violently that Court felt certain he'd break his fool neck.

"I want you to go to your room and stay put. If I come in that room and you're not doing exactly as I say, you will be sorry." He shoved the kid away before the urge to leave a more lasting impression overwhelmed Court. "Now, apologize."

Charlie looked from Court to Sabrina. "Sorry," he muttered. "I didn't mean what I said." He turned sharply and ran up the stairs. A door slammed soon afterward.

Sabrina started after him, but Court stayed her. "Let him go. He's embarrassed that I showed him up. He won't want to talk to you right now."

She turned to Court. "That man, Ferguson, really intended to do Charlie harm?"

Court nodded. "I'm sure of it. I think he planned it to get at me. He's all bent out of shape about the relationship between Neely and me."

Sabrina wet her lips. "He came here this afternoon."

Her words shook Court. "What do you mean, he came here?"

"When I got home from Mrs. Cartwright's, he was waiting for me. He saw me leave your room this morning. He said he was watching you." Her tears had dried, but she swiped nervously at the dampness on her cheeks. "I think he suspects you're a cop or something."

"Did he say that?" Court demanded. Ferguson's suspicion really wasn't anything Court hadn't expected, but he hated like hell that Ferguson had grown so cocky so quickly.

"He said something like he didn't think you were

who or what you appeared." She shrugged tiredly. "I'm sorry. I was so scared, I barely paid attention. I was afraid he would—" Her eyes widened with remembered fear.

"Did he touch you?" Court barely recognized the voice as his own. If Ferguson laid one hand on her he was a dead man.

She shook her head. "He just acted strangely and I was frightened."

The baby twisted his little head around, trying to see Court, but Sabrina kept pressing him back to her chest. Those same old questions jumped back to the forefront of his mind. Why had she kept her baby a secret from him? When had she married? No, Charlie had called the child a bastard. She hadn't married. Court didn't know that much about babies, but he was pretty sure this one was a year or so old. Add to that nine months and he came up with a number just shy of two years. He stilled. Two years. He and Sabrina had been together two years ago. The night after his mother's funeral. And, like this time, they'd both been too needy and unthinking to use protection. They'd made love twice that night.

Court lifted his gaze from the squirming child to Sabrina. A new kind of fear stared back at him from those dark brown eyes. She was afraid. Not of Ferguson, not of Charlie's threats. She was afraid of Court.

"This is my child?" he demanded, the breath going out of him at hearing his own question spoken aloud. "Ryan—" Court gestured vaguely "—is my son?"

She nodded, the movement barely visible. Renewed tears slipped down her cheeks.

Court's gaze moved back to the child. He had a son. A *son*. And she hadn't bothered to tell him. Court felt his head move from side to side in denial, then the question tumbled out of his mouth. "Why?" His expectant gaze latched onto hers. He had to know why.

Her lower lip quivered. She sucked in an unsteady breath in an effort to find her composure. "Because you didn't want me or this place. You only wanted away from here. I didn't want to trap you into coming back."

What kind of excuse was that? Court's eyes watered. He scrubbed at them impatiently with the heels of his hands. The conversations they had shared that night between lovemaking sessions arrowed into his head in rapid-fire succession. He'd told her how much he loved the Bureau. How he was so glad to be away from Montana, that he never wanted to come back. Something heavy weighted down his shoulders at the memories. He'd been totally arrogant about it, too. He'd taken the comfort she offered and bragged about how he wouldn't be back here. That nothing could bring him back. Not even her, he realized. He swallowed at the emotions clogging his throat. Not even his son. The one she decided not to tell him about.

"You should have told me." His shocked frustration and self-disgust rechanneled into anger. "You had no right to keep him from me."

Ryan tugged at his mother's hair. Something in her gaze changed, hardened. "I took the right," she challenged. "You walked away, you wanted no part of this place. I had every right."

Court resisted the urge to pace. He tossed his hat onto

a nearby chair and plowed his fingers through his hair. When his gaze reconnected with hers, he had his emotions back under some semblance of control. "Even after last night, you weren't going to tell me?"

She lifted her chin defiantly. "Why should I? You're still planning to leave. I don't want my son to be hurt the way you hurt me."

Her words twisted the knife of regret already buried deeply in his chest. "You think I would do anything to hurt my own child?"

Her eyes gave him her answer. Yes. Yes, she did. He shook his head. How could she think that? "Then you don't know me at all."

"I know you, Court Brody, too well," she argued, stepping closer, her anger shoring up her courage. "I know you better than you know yourself. You've run from your past your entire adult life. You're not going to stop now, not for me or for Ryan. Don't let the urge to possess what you think simple biology makes yours slow you down. I don't want Ryan to become attached to you, and then have you walk out on him like you did me. You have to earn the right to be a father. You should know that better than anyone."

Court looked away. He hadn't run. He just hadn't wanted to be here. He'd left because he hated the place. His life was somewhere else. And how could she compare him to his father? He was nothing like his old man. Nothing at all. Except he'd hurt the people who cared about him most. His own mother, when he, like his older brothers, refused to stay in Montana. And Sabrina, when he'd left her behind. Maybe he was like his father. Dammit. But she hadn't given him the chance to prove he could do better.

"You should have given me the opportunity," he said, countering her accusations. He had rights. "You couldn't have known how I would react."

"I wasn't willing to take the risk," she replied. "I might take chances with my own heart, but I won't do it with Ryan's."

The baby made a sound, something between a sigh and a whine. In spite of the emotions churning inside him, Court smiled at the sound. This was his son. "I want to hold him." He held out his arms. "Please."

Hesitation slowed her. Court could see the doubt in her eyes, but she passed the baby to him, anyway. Ryan squirmed, peering up at the stranger holding him. Court was certain the child would break out into a fit of crying, but he didn't. He blinked, his little lids heavy. Maybe he was too sleepy to put up a fuss. Or maybe he was just curious. His eyes were gray just like Court's. His hair a little darker, but not much. Ryan touched Court's face with chubby fingers and Court's heart shuddered. This was his son.

The notion that Ferguson had come anywhere near this house, near his son, and Sabrina, shifted something dark and primal inside Court. His arms tightened around the child, making him fuss and squirm.

Sabrina reached for her baby, the same uncertainty warring inside Court clear in her eyes. "I should put him to bed now and check on Charlie. Ryan's usually asleep by now," she explained when Court hesitated.

Court relinquished his hold on his son, knowing that

Sabrina was right. "I'll just be outside," he told her as she hurried from the room. From him.

Weak with the receding adrenaline that accompanied tonight's discoveries, Court walked out onto the porch and sat down on the top step. He peered up at the clear sky and the stars shining brightly down and wondered how everything could look the same when nothing was. The crescent moon winked at him from amid the brilliant stars.

He had a son. He did the math again. A son who was fifteen months old and didn't know his father. Fury lashed anew within him. How could she keep his child a secret from him for more than a year? Didn't she know that he would never walk out on his responsibilities? Court surveyed all that lay before him. The realization that Sabrina had suffered through childbirth alone, through hanging on to this ranch by the skin of her teeth mocked him, and all along he could have helped her. Could have been there for her when Ryan was born.

But she hadn't given him that chance. When they'd made love this morning, he'd felt closer to her than any other human being on earth, and yet she had held this secret from him. How did she plan to survive trying to run this ranch alone and raising their child? Did she trust him so little that she would endure anything to keep the truth from him?

Sabrina stepped out onto the porch to face Court's wrath. Whatever he had to say to her, she doubted it would be good. She hadn't missed the accusing look in his eyes. She had expected it. And maybe even deserved it a little. But she'd done what she did to protect her son…and Court to an extent. He had been adamant about leaving Montana once and for all. Telling him about Ryan would only have made him feel obligated to stay.

"They're both asleep," she announced as she paused at the railing and leaned against it, keeping a safe distance from the man staring out at nothing at all.

"When you made love with me this morning," he began, his gaze somewhere in the distance, his voice strangely emotionless, "when we held each other afterward, how could you not tell me the truth?" He lifted his gaze to hers then, and she saw the devastation she had caused. Her heart bled at the sight. "I risked my cover—my life—by telling you the truth. And still, you kept my son from me."

A burst of anger shored up her waning courage. "If I'd called you up a couple of months after you left and said, hey, guess what, I'm pregnant, would you have come running back here?" She shook her head before he could answer. "I don't think so. You didn't want any part of this place. You still don't. This is my home, Ryan's home. If you don't want any part of the place, how can you want us?"

Ire flickered in his smoky eyes. "I had a right to know. You were wrong to keep him from me, Brin. Don't try to pretend you don't realize that. Admit it," he demanded.

She folded her arms over her middle. "Maybe I was wrong, but it was the decision I made based on what I knew about you."

He pushed to his feet, his posture rigid. "That's a cop-out if I've ever heard one."

"You weren't here, Court. You don't have a clue what I went through then or how I made my decisions."

He stepped up onto the porch, closer to her. "That's right, I wasn't here. Because you didn't give me that chance. You took it away from me to punish me for leaving."

Disbelief, so profound, flooded her; she couldn't speak for a full five seconds. "Punish you? Get real, Court. I had survival on my mind. I sure as hell didn't have time to worry about how I could get back at you." Or had she? The question came from so deep inside her that it made her jerk with surprise. She hadn't purposely set out to punish Court...had she? Had some small part of her wanted to keep Ryan a secret in hopes of kicking Court in the teeth with the revelation some day? Sabrina suddenly remembered thinking those very words just recently, but she couldn't have consciously decided that back then. Too much was going on in her life.

She glared at him. He was putting all the blame on her and ignoring his own actions. "Besides, if you'd stuck around a little while you would have known."

It always came down to him leaving. She knew it. And so did he.

"It's my fault. I left, so I guess that means that I lost the right to my son?"

Sabrina wanted to shout "that's right," but it wasn't that simple. He was trying to break it down to an uncomplicated decision and that just wasn't the case.

"It wasn't that simple," she argued. "Don't try to put words in my mouth."

He moved closer still. The memory of his intimate

touch, of the way he'd made love to her before daylight, made her hot and restless. She wanted to back up a step, but her body wouldn't let her.

"We could argue this point all night," he said quietly, his tone suddenly calm. "But it's not getting us anywhere and I have to get back to the compound before Ferguson comes looking for me."

"He knows you're here?" None of them would be safe with that man lurking about.

"He saw me leave with Charlie. I can guarantee you he's madder than hell because I messed up his little plans for tonight. I have to get back and run interference. He might go to Neely with his suspicions."

That thought sent a chill spiraling through Sabrina. "What are you going to do? Are you sure it's safe to go back?" The possibility of Court being hurt scared her to death.

"I have to go back."

He wasn't answering her question. A bad sign. "Is it safe for you to go back?" she repeated.

He hesitated. "Probably. At least for now."

A tiny sprout of relief took root near her heart. "What if he comes here looking for you again?"

"You won't be here," Court explained. "I want you to take Charlie and Ryan to the Lonesome Pony. Tell Austin I sent you."

"The Lonesome Pony?" She frowned her confusion. Why would she go there? How did Court know Mr. Austin?

"Trust me, Brin. You go there tonight and stay there until this is over."

"But what if Charlie won't go?" she asked, suddenly remembering the grim reality that he didn't listen to her anymore.

"If Charlie gives you one millisecond of trouble, you call Austin and tell him to come pick him up."

She shook her head, completely bewildered now. "What's Austin got to do with this?"

"I can't explain. Just do as I say. Austin will keep the three of you safe until this is over. He knows what's going down. I've already talked to him," Court assured her.

Court was going back to the compound alone. Neely, Ferguson and all those faithful followers would be against Court if any of them suspected…

"Who's going to protect you?"

Court gave her one of those lopsided smiles. "I can take care of myself."

Panic twisted inside her. "Don't go back, Court. I'm afraid for you." Tears stung her eyes. She couldn't bear it if something happened to him. No matter that he likely hated her now that he knew her secret. She loved him.

She loved him.

The words echoed through her soul. She didn't want him to be hurt.

"I have to go back." He fixed her with a gaze that gave nothing of his own feelings away. "We'll settle this when I return. Ryan is my son. I want him in my life."

Sabrina could only nod. A mixture of fear, panic and pain had a stranglehold on her ability to speak.

"Keep your rifle handy, just in case," he suggested, hesitance and uncertainty flickering in his gaze. "Can I see him one more time before I go? I mean, if it's all right. I just want to see him."

Feeling as if she were in a kind of shock, Sabrina led the way to the first-floor bedroom. The one her parents had always used. Ryan's crib sat in the far corner. The lamp on the bedside table cast a dim glow over the room. Court stood next to her, his gaze never leaving his son. Emotion slipped down her cheeks in warm, salty rivulets.

"Can I kiss him good-night?"

Without meeting Court's gaze, Sabrina quietly lowered the side rail so that he could reach his son. Her baby lay sleeping on his tummy. His sweet face turned toward them. His silky hair dark against the yellow sheets.

Court leaned down and gently kissed his son's soft head. Sabrina's heart squeezed at the sight. Dear God, had she made a mistake?

If so, she could only hope that Court would not make her pay for that mistake now.

Surely he would not demand custody of his son. But he could. Financially, her life was falling apart. Every day the ranch fell more deeply into disrepair. And Charlie was practically a juvenile delinquent. But Sabrina knew he was just acting out against all he'd suffered in his life. Losing his father, and then his mother. Sabrina was all he'd had. And tonight, with his outburst, she'd realized why he resented Ryan so very much. Charlie saw Ryan as taking the only family he had left away from him. Somehow she had to make her brother see that she loved them both.

Court turned to her then, his eyes void of any emotion at all, his voice empty when he spoke. "Do exactly what I told you, Brin. I'll be back when I can."

Then he left.

Sabrina stared at the door.

Court would never forgive her for keeping Ryan from him.

Never.

CHAPTER TEN

THE MOMENT COURT entered the compound gate, he knew something was wrong. The place was eerily quiet. Though it was after dark, it wasn't that late. Not past lockdown. Other than the guard at the gate and his Uzi, nothing moved. Court parked his truck and slid from behind the wheel. The observation towers, he noted as he scanned the area, were manned with one guard as usual. He reached for the weapon beneath his seat and tucked it into the waistband of his jeans at the small of his back. There was no way to know what Ferguson had done since he left or to know what he might have told Neely.

But Court would deal with the situation one step at a time. If he lived long enough. He'd been in the business too long to take his next breath for granted.

As he strode toward the training center a sound from the meeting hall snagged his attention. He stilled, listening. He could just make out the sound of applause, cheers and shouts. The lights were on in the building, sending bright rectangles of golden light into the dark night. There hadn't been a rally planned for tonight as far as Court could recall. But obviously something had come up.

Slowly, being careful to note any other sound or movement around him, Court headed in the direction of the meeting hall. The closer he got, the louder the thundering applause and savage war cries. Bracing himself for whatever he had to face, Court eased the door open and slipped inside.

The hall was filled to capacity. Standing room only. Men, women and children were standing, cheering and clapping at Neely's every pause. The sounds reverberated inside Court, edging his tension to a higher level.

"We shall end the oppression. Tomorrow is the beginning," Neely boomed from the podium.

Another exhilarated roar rolled over the excited crowd. Tomorrow? Court studied Neely and several of the lieutenants who stood near him. What the hell was going on tomorrow? Had something new developed in the hour or so he'd been gone? A disturbing feeling crept into Court's gut. Maybe he was the new development.

A strong hand clamped down on his shoulder. Court went rigid with expectation. He turned to face what would no doubt be one or more of the guards.

"Where the hell have you been, buddy?" Raymond shouted over the revelry of the crowd. "I've been watching for you to get back for almost an hour. Then the rally started and I had to come inside. We gotta go up there." He nodded toward the stage where Neely and the rest of the leaders stood.

Without giving Court the opportunity to ask questions or to even respond, Raymond headed toward the front of the hall. Court followed, weaving through the throng of worked-up militia members. Whatever was about to go down, Court had a very bad feeling that he wasn't going to like it.

Ferguson glanced in Court's direction when he stepped in next to Raymond. Court held the man's gaze for several seconds, but read nothing in his eyes. When Ferguson turned back to the crowd before them, a smile had widened across his face. Court couldn't be sure if the smile was about him or simply for the onlookers.

"With these more powerful weapons we will fight the oppressors for the rights of our brothers," Neely promised his faithful onlookers. "We will finally stand up against those who would tell us how we will live on our own land."

A chorus of heartfelt agreement echoed through the hall.

"Now," Neely continued, the one word bringing absolute silence to the room, "at dawn our shipment of arms will arrive…."

Court tensed. At dawn? Fahey wasn't supposed to deliver the goods until day after tomorrow.

"I need twelve good, strong men in addition to my lieutenants who are prepared to make this journey with us." He held up his hand to stay the overenthusiastic crowd. "I cannot in good conscience accept volunteers without first warning you that this mission, though vital to the cause, is very dangerous. Do not volunteer to go with us unless you are prepared to die for the cause."

Members surged forward, pressing against the stage, crying out for Neely's attention. Court scanned the faces of those who showed their readiness to follow Neely into death if necessary. Court had to find a way to get word to Austin. He couldn't let this buy go down with no backup.

"Lieutenants—" Neely turned to face the men on his

right "—each of you shall choose one man to accompany our team this night. We must leave in a few short hours." He stepped away from the podium, an unspoken command to begin.

As each man passed on his way off the stage, Neely shook his hand, embracing some as if they were about to go off to war. When Court reached him, Neely smiled.

"Brother Brody."

Court clasped his hand. "Joshua."

Neely pulled Court into a tight embrace. Court forced his body to relax completely, so as not to give away his mounting tension.

"Are you prepared to die for me, Court?" Neely murmured.

Court drew back and looked the man squarely in the eyes. "I'm prepared to do whatever you need me to do, Joshua."

One of those charismatic, politician-type smiles slid across Neely's face. "I have complete faith, Brother Brody, that you will, in fact, do just that."

Uncertain as to whether Neely's words carried some hidden meaning, Court moved on, allowing the lieutenant behind him to receive Neely's blessing. Once Court had descended from the stage, he scanned the expectant faces around him. He had to choose a man from this mob, one whose life might be lost if there was trouble at dawn. The whole exchange could go down without a glitch. But there was no way to be sure. Somehow Court had to get word to Austin that the deal was going down ahead of schedule.

Clydus Beecham pushed his way through the throng

and stood directly in front of Court. "I'm your man," he announced, his back ramrod straight, his camouflage uniform wrinkled from too many days of wear without a wash.

Court hesitated. He didn't want to be the cause of any man walking into a death trap. But he had to choose. Beecham was a die-hard Neely follower. Hell, if Court didn't pick him someone else probably would.

He nodded finally. "All right, Beecham." He slapped the man on the back and produced a smile. "You'll do fine."

Beecham whooped and jumped clear off the floor. Court glanced to his left to find Ferguson watching him. Ferguson looked away too quickly. Instinct warned Court that Ferg was up to something. The first thing Court needed to do was find out what had happened while he was at Sabrina's. Moving up Fahey's schedule couldn't have been easy—there had to be big-time motivation. *Unless Fahey moved the schedule up himself.* That was a possibility, but every fiber of Court's being warned him that there was more to it than that.

Court pushed past the clutch of volunteers in front of him and threaded his way to Raymond at the fringes of the crowd. He tapped his friend on the shoulder and Raymond turned toward him. Raymond would know the deal.

"What happened?" Court asked. "I thought we were on with Fahey for day after tomorrow."

Raymond pulled him to the side. "Joshua got word that the ATF planned to send in another mole. He figured he'd better get this done now." Raymond's expression turned angry. "Bastards think they can stop us. I hope I get to kill the next fed in our midst." He grinned at

Court. "Hell, Joshua let you take care of Benson. Didn't it feel—" Raymond shrugged at his obvious inability to put his feelings into words "—hell, I don't know, *liberating* to put a bullet in that bastard's head?"

Court nodded as if he understood exactly what Raymond meant. To slow the building disgust that threatened to overwhelm him, Court allowed the image of his son sleeping so peacefully in his crib to fill his mind one last time, then he stored it away.

Right now he had to focus on the mission. As he surveyed the room once more, his gaze locked with Neely's. The look that passed between them was unexpectedly revealing and oddly calming.

Court had been made.

SABRINA PACED THE FLOOR for more than half an hour trying to decide what to do. How could she just show up at Austin's? What did he have to do with any of this? How could she think when Court had gone back to the compound knowing that an ambush might be waiting for him? He had risked his life to bring Charlie home to her.

And now he knew about Ryan.

Sabrina retraced her path, in the opposite direction. She'd seen the hurt in his eyes. He would never forgive her for keeping that secret. She'd been wrong to do it. Sabrina rubbed her eyes wearily. She'd thought it was the right thing at the time. Court would surely have felt trapped.

Or would he? She thought she knew all there was to know about Court, but she was obviously wrong. Though she knew Court was a good man, an honorable man, she hadn't known until tonight how far he would go—just how much he would sacrifice—for someone else. He'd put his life on the line for Charlie. And for her, just last night. Any man who was willing to give his own life for another would do the right thing by his own son.

Sabrina collapsed into the nearest chair. Court would have done right by her and by Ryan, had she only given him the chance. She closed her eyes and restrained the tears. God, she'd made a terrible mistake. Not one that had cost her, not really, but one that had cost Court…and Ryan. She opened her eyes and took a deep breath. She'd hurt Court and their son by keeping her secret. She'd been wounded, her heart broken, and she'd selfishly chosen the one path that would ensure that Court would be repaid in spades. But she'd been wrong.

So very wrong.

Sabrina pushed out of her chair. She had to check on Charlie and Ryan. One way or another she had to keep Charlie safe until she decided what to do. She rolled Daniel's name over and over in her head, considering how he fit into all this. She had no way of knowing. She only knew that he had helped her in the past. Could she turn to him now, for this? And Court had insisted she go to Austin.

Moving quietly, she mounted the stairs and eased soundlessly into Charlie's room. He was asleep. At rest, he looked like the little boy she'd been left to raise. Had she done such a bad job that he couldn't stand the sight of her now? Sabrina's chest ached to have the relationship with her baby brother that she'd once had. How could things have gone so wrong so fast?

Deciding to stay here the night, and careful not to

wake Charlie, Sabrina slipped back into the hall. She descended the stairs, other thoughts whirling inside her. She'd made so many mistakes with Charlie and Ryan. How would she ever right all these wrongs? She prayed that she would have a second chance with Charlie.

And a second chance with Court.

But somehow she doubted the latter. How could Court ever trust her again? Though he hadn't blown up completely and threatened to take Ryan from her, time had been short. He'd had to get back to the compound. After he'd had time to think about what she'd done, how would he feel then?

Sabrina pushed the agonizing thoughts away and peeked in on her baby. She smiled down at him. He was so beautiful. His silky hair ruffled, his lips pursed in sleep, probably dreaming of nursing. She'd loved the feel of him at her breast so much that she hadn't weaned him until a couple of months ago. He still snuggled against her, but didn't fret when he realized that Mommy wasn't going to offer him nourishment or comfort in that manner any longer.

Okay, Sabrina, lay down your tired head and close your eyes. She knew she couldn't sleep if she didn't at least try. In the morning she would go talk to Austin. She shuffled back to the living room and reached to turn out the light when a soft knock at the front door stopped her.

Fear shot through her. What if Neely's men were here now, looking for her? Maybe she should have listened to Court. The soft knock sounded again. Sabrina forced herself to be calm. If it were Ferguson or one of his bunch they'd simply kick the door down.

Shoring up her shaky bravado, Sabrina peeked out the window to look for a vehicle. The outside light cast a large pool of light over the driveway directly in front of the house. Sabrina frowned when she found no vehicle out front. Could someone have parked farther down the drive? Someone who wanted to hide their identity until it was too late and she'd already opened the door? Fear tightened its grip on her. She moistened her lips and eased closer to the door. If whoever was out there decided to knock louder they might wake Ryan. She didn't want that. But she needed to get her rifle like Court had told her before she opened that door.

"Sabrina, it's me," a frail voice called out.

Mrs. Cartwright?

Sabrina quickly unbolted and jerked the door open. "What are you doing out at this time of night?"

"I was worried about you, dear." Mrs. Cartwright looked as white as a sheet and feebler than Sabrina had ever seen her look before.

She peered out the door, past the stooped woman's shoulder. "How did you get here?"

Mrs. Cartwright smiled, the gesture triumphant and a little wicked. "Why, I drove, of course. I parked my car around back by your truck, just like I used to."

Sabrina's eyes rounded. "But the doctor said you weren't to drive anymore. What if—"

The elderly lady made a sound of dismissal. "That old goat doesn't know everything. It didn't hurt a thing for me to drive over here."

Sabrina ushered her inside and closed and rebolted the door. "Why didn't you just call? We're fine here."

Mrs. Cartwright waved a frail hand. "Fool phone quit on me again. I should never have bought one of those no good cordless things. They're too much trouble."

Sabrina offered a patient smile. The poor old lady had likely left the handset off the base too long like she had the last time. Now it wouldn't work again until it recharged. "What made you think something was wrong?" she asked, worried that Mrs. Cartwright would take off in the middle of the night when the doctor had given strict orders that she wasn't to be driving. Jeez, just what she needed, Mrs. Cartwright keeling over with a heart attack from worrying about her.

"Don't you remember, dear, you were supposed to bring Ryan to me tonight. I waited and waited. When you didn't come I was sure something was wrong."

Sabrina closed her eyes and sighed, disgusted with herself. She had thought she might have to go back to the compound. "I'm sorry, my plans changed." She didn't bother going into the details. She couldn't talk about that right now. It was too hard…too much hung in the balance.

"That's all right, dear. I was just worried, that's all. If everything is fine here, I'll go on back home."

Sabrina shook her head at that suggestion. "I'd feel better if you stayed here tonight."

"Oh, I couldn't do that. I haven't slept anywhere but in my own bed in over fifty years."

"Please," Sabrina pleaded. "I don't want you to go back out tonight."

Mrs. Cartwright's eyes were too knowing. "What is it you're not telling me, Sabrina?"

"We may be in danger. Court's worried about something that's supposed to happen with Neely and his men in a couple of days."

"Oh, Lordy." The older woman's face grew even paler. "I knew this would be the way of it when that charlatan came into town almost two years ago."

Sabrina nodded her agreement. "You can go with us to the Lonesome Pony in the morning. Court said we'd be safe there. Daniel Austin is his friend." She didn't see any point in mentioning that Court had wanted them to go tonight.

Mrs. Cartwright took Sabrina's hand and patted it gently. "That's what we'll do, then. We'll go together. It's about time I found out what I've been missing by not sleeping someplace different."

A smile spread across Sabrina's face. She felt better already. Everything was going to be fine. Court said he'd done this before. He could take care of himself. All she had to do was keep Ryan and Charlie safe. And Mrs. Cartwright.

Sabrina showed Mrs. Cartwright to her bedroom. She felt certain the stairs would be too much. Sabrina could sleep on the couch. "You can sleep in here with Ryan," she offered.

"I always keep a glass of water on the table," Mrs. Cartwright said hesitantly. "Could I have some water, dear?"

"Of course." Leaving the elderly woman to prepare for bed, Sabrina switched off the living room light as she headed to the kitchen. She finally felt as if she might be able to sleep, herself. Without switching on the kitchen light, she located a glass and filled it with cool tap water. Everything was going to be fine, she told herself again.

Just as she was halfway through the living room on her way back to Mrs. Cartwright, headlights flashed across the front window, stopping Sabrina dead in her tracks. She raced to the window, water sloshing, and peered past the edge of the curtain and through the open window. The warm, gentle breeze brushed against her cheeks. She quickly recognized the vehicle Ferguson had driven earlier that day. Terror snaked around her heart. Voices sounded as several men climbed out of the truck.

She dropped the glass of water. It crashed on the floor, sending water and shards of glass across the hardwood. Sabrina skirted the debris and ran for the bedroom. "They're here. I have to hide you and the baby. *Now.*"

Mrs. Cartwright's gaze connected with hers for an instant before the danger registered. "Where can we hide?"

"In the old fruit cellar." Sabrina grabbed her sleeping child and hurried across the dark living room and into the kitchen, Mrs. Cartwright on her heels. She skirted the dining table and kicked aside the edge of the oversize area rug that extended from beneath it. She passed Ryan to Mrs. Cartwright and threw open the old wooden trap door. She assisted the elderly woman down the steps.

"What about you?" Mrs. Cartwright asked worriedly. Fear glittered in her eyes as she held Ryan protectively in her arms.

"I'll be fine. I have to get Charlie. Just, please, keep Ryan quiet and don't come out no matter what happens until you're sure they're gone."

Mrs. Cartwright held on when Sabrina would have turned away. "Take care, child."

Sabrina nodded, then dashed up the steps. Why hadn't she listened to Court? She closed the door and covered it once more when she heard the first crash against the front door. She hurried to the living room and turned on the light. She glanced at the second-story landing and prayed that Charlie would wake up and hide. The front door burst open just as she reached for it.

"I told you I'd be watching you," Ferguson said, sneering as he led a group of three men into her living room.

"What do you want?" she demanded, her voice steadier than she would have expected.

"Why, I want you, sweetheart, didn't you know?" The other men tittered with laughter. "Neely sent me. He requires your presence." Ferguson snickered. "Now, where's that skinny little brother of yours?"

"I don't know where he is. He didn't come home tonight." She folded her arms over her chest and gave Ferguson her best glare. She prayed with all her heart that Ryan would not wake up and start to cry. *Please, God,* she prayed *protect them all.*

"Search the house," Ferguson barked to his men. "Leave no stone unturned," he added in true Joshua Neely fashion.

Sabrina held her breath as two of the men bounded up the stairs and the other stomped around downstairs. Her heart threatened to burst from her chest. She held her breath as one man circled the kitchen, opening cabinet doors and slamming them shut. *Please, please don't let my baby wake up,* she prayed again. She kept expecting to hear Charlie's voice, but it never came. She frowned with a new worry. Could he have sneaked out of his room without her knowing it? Or maybe her prayer was answered and he was hiding.

When the banging of doors and furniture and the stamping of heavy boots finally ceased, Ferguson was fit to be tied.

"Where is the damn kid?" he demanded in reference to Charlie.

Sabrina looked at him and said slowly, succinctly, "I don't know. He isn't here." Despite her lack of knowledge of Charlie's whereabouts, she felt relieved that these men had not found him. He had to have sneaked out his bedroom window. Wherever he was, she hoped he didn't go near that militia compound.

Ferguson nudged the tip of his weapon beneath her chin. "Your boyfriend left the compound with him just before dark. I figured he was coming here. To deliver your little brother and maybe have some more fun with you." A round of vulgar chuckles passed through the men gathered around him.

"I haven't seen Court, and I have no idea where Charlie is. I thought he was at the compound," she lied without wavering.

"Well, not to worry. We'll find Charlie boy. We've got Mr. Court Brody figured out, too," Ferguson said with glee. "We know he's a fed. Hell, I tried to tell Joshua when he fingered Benson that it was too big a coincidence. But he wouldn't listen at first. But then, you see, word got back to Joshua that his plans were being leaked and we both knew Brody had to be the one. So we changed our plans."

Sabrina's heart stilled. They were going to kill Court. "You can't be sure," she argued.

"Oh, we made a positive ID, as the cops say." Ferguson gave her one of his disgusting grins. "But you see, we're one step ahead of dear old Court. We're gonna do our deal at dawn tomorrow while his people are waiting until the day after. By then Court Brody will be history."

"Dead meat," one of the others chimed in.

"We don't tolerate traitors," Ferguson added. He snagged her by the arm. "And, as far as I can tell, you're in cahoots with him, so that makes you a traitor in my book."

Sabrina tried to free herself from his hold. "Let me go!" She kicked at his shins, but he only laughed at her. She stopped fighting then. She needed to get them out of her house before Ryan awoke. Let them take her. At least her baby would be safe with Mrs. Cartwright.

"Come on." Ferguson dragged her toward the door. "You and your boyfriend can meet your Maker together."

Sabrina blinked back the tears as she allowed Ferguson to drag her out the door. They were leaving the house and that's all that mattered.

She only wished there was some way she could warn Court and Charlie.

CHAPTER ELEVEN

THE SKY PINKED with dawn as Court stepped out of the jeep at the scheduled rendezvous point. Raymond killed the engine and scanned the area as if expecting something he didn't see, then climbed out as well. He hadn't said much of anything since their journey had begun just more than four hours ago. The silence proved more telling than anything the man could have said. Court already knew the verdict, he'd seen it in Neely's eyes last night.

Beecham and another of Neely's soldiers, whose name Court couldn't remember at the moment, scrambled from the rear of the jungle-green jeep. The entourage looked like a group of National Guardsmen, complete with camouflage uniforms, who had found themselves lost in the woods. Well, except for the car that had hung way back from the convoy during the long journey. The windows were tinted so Court couldn't make out the faces of the passengers or the driver.

Only a few miles from Canada and the Blackfeet Reservation, the view was an awesome one, despite the circumstances that brought Court here. The Rocky Mountains rose in the distance, everything in between sleeping in their shadow. He sure wouldn't find a wide-open blue sky or a breathtaking view like this in D.C. It was a shame that they had come to such a beautiful place to do their dirty work. A lone eagle flew over the wilderness terrain, suspect, no doubt, of the one car, three jeeps and two supply trucks sitting amid the soaring pines.

Court took a long, deep draw of the fresh, clean air. No matter how he denied his feelings, Montana was still home in an elemental way over which he had no control. His past, Sabrina, Ryan, his only true heart-and-soul connections to this world were right there on that ranch he'd so despised as a kid. And he'd waited too late to realize it, for any minute now all chance of righting that wrong would be taken from him. Neely's sense of irony seemed a bit overdone. Surely he realized that Court sensed his impending demise.

And that just made it more exhilarating for Neely.

Ferguson barked a steady stream of orders to several of the men unloading from the vehicles, instructing them to fan out around the clearing and take cover in the edge of the woods. The others were ordered to take up posts around the two empty trucks. Neely sat in the jeep Ferguson had driven, watching his men scurry as they followed orders.

"I think there's more coffee in the thermos if you want some," Raymond offered, coming to stand alongside Court.

For a moment Court studied the man who had befriended him, then shook his head. Was he feeling any regret? "No, thanks, I'm good."

Raymond's usually easy smile was forced. Court

wondered if Neely would kill Raymond, too. After all, it was Raymond who had brought Court into their tight circle. Court hoped like hell they didn't. None of this was Raymond's fault, he was nothing but a pawn in Neely's demented plan.

Court next wondered how long it would be before Austin figured out something was wrong…if he did. Would Neely set up some sort of ambush for when Austin showed up tomorrow, or would he simply allow them to find nothing out here but the trees and tranquillity God intended? Court hoped for the latter. By noon today the deal would be done, Court would be dead, his body disposed of, and Neely and his arms would be back at the compound. And no one would be able to prove anything.

Court considered his only option. He could manage to get close enough to Neely—use him for leverage— in an attempt to stop the exchange. Maybe he should just kill the bastard and be done with it. Raymond leaned against the hood of the truck, only a couple of feet away from Court. These men would never allow Court that close to Neely. Not now. And, the truth was, he still needed Neely and whatever information he stored in that warped brain of his.

Court didn't know how he'd been made, but he knew he had. Although Neely had obviously ordered the men closest to him to carry on with the charade, since Court was still armed and seemingly a part of the mission, Raymond hung too close and Ferguson kept his hawk-eyed gaze glued to Court. If Court made one wrong move it would end now.

He had no choice but to allow the scene to play out and see where it ended. Barring a miracle, he was dead one way or the other, but there was no point in hastening the event. And Court was a firm believer in the motto that it wasn't over until it was over. Hell, he could get lucky. The world could end in the next five minutes. Yeah, right. Court scrubbed a hand over his jaw. The only thing he could do was pay attention and take his best shot at getting out of this situation if the opportunity presented itself.

They would disarm him first, he reasoned, then make an example of him to the others. The twelve volunteers who'd been chosen to take part in today's little adventure would rush back to the compound with the news, thus discouraging future betrayal.

Neely made everything work to his advantage. Though he undoubtedly felt like a horse's ass for trusting Court in the first place, he would turn it around to cast the best light upon himself.

The other thoughts and memories he'd kept at bay all night suddenly came flooding back. Court had a son. A son who would never know him if Neely had his way. Court hoped Sabrina was making preparations to get them to safety. Once this mission was over, Ferguson might just do something really stupid like trying to hurt Sabrina or Charlie. The kid had been pretty rough on his sister last night. Court hated that he might not be there to help set the kid straight when this was over. But more than anything, the thought that he wouldn't be able to help raise his son knifed deep into his gut.

He'd spent pretty much the entire journey contemplating the things he'd done wrong in his life. And there were plenty. Most especially the way he'd treated Sabrina in the past. She'd been a part of his life for as long as he could remember. He'd watched her grow up, and he'd known that she loved him. Oh, he'd tried to pretend that it was just a crush, but deep down he'd known better. Twice he had taken advantage of those feelings, both times pretending that though he cared for her, it wasn't anything to make a big deal over. He'd justified his actions by rationalizing the situation down to a matter of lust.

But he'd been wrong.

His mistake had put Sabrina on the offensive. She had protected herself and her baby the only way she knew how, by eliminating Court from her life. When he'd showed up here again, she'd been frantic to keep her secret safe. Only it seemed that her heart wouldn't let her push Court completely away. And, like always, he'd been ready and willing to take advantage of the situation.

God, he was a jerk. Though what Sabrina had done was wrong, he definitely couldn't put all the blame on her shoulders. In one long burst Court exhaled the breath he'd been holding. He had a lot of damage control to take care of—he surveyed the militant group around him, his gaze eventually landing on Neely—if he got the chance.

A shout of warning echoed from the advance scout Ferguson had positioned on the slight rise in the dirt road that led into the clearing. Fahey was coming. As Court moved to attention, he recalled his son's angelic face and then that of Sabrina's once more before storing them carefully away. The next few minutes would require all of his attention and cunning. Somehow he had to find a way to get back to Sabrina…to somehow make things right for his son. For all of them.

A large panel truck sporting a moving company logo rounded the bend in the road and entered the clearing where Court and the others waited. Two men, armed with Uzis, climbed down from the cab of the truck. Both quickly approached Neely.

"You have the money?" one inquired by way of a greeting.

"Where's Fahey?" Neely returned, cool, composed.

"When I see the money," the man said with a smile that was neither a gesture of amusement or friendliness.

Neely nodded to Ferguson, who quickly produced two steel briefcases from the back seat of the jeep. After inspecting the contents of the two cases, the man removed the two-way radio from his belt and gave the go-ahead to Fahey.

In anticipation of the other man's arrival, Neely stepped down from the jeep and readied to meet him. Another panel truck, this one marked with the advertisement of a Canadian furniture company, followed by a black SUV, entered the area. Court recognized Fahey when he stepped from the SUV. Though he'd never seen the man in person, the arms dealer's face was easily identified from the photographs in his Bureau file. Olive coloring, dark hair, but the really distinguishing feature was the scar that slashed his jaw from the corner of his left eye to his mouth. This was the mark of his one up-close encounter with a federal under-cover agent.

Once the formalities were out of the way, the transfer of cash and the shaking of hands, the work began. The weapons were stored inside specially designed couches, rather than the typical transport crates. Court wondered how many border inspectors this ruse had fooled. Neely's trucks contained storage crates for careful transport of the new weapons. Court worked alongside Raymond and the other lieutenants to transfer the weapons. The rest of the men remained at their posts, just to be sure Fahey's entourage didn't make any unexpected moves.

It didn't take long to get the job done. Court removed his hat and wiped the perspiration from his brow, then reached behind him to adjust the Beretta tucked in his waistband. He settled his hat back into place and scanned the faces around him. Court needed to get close to Neely. Taking anyone else hostage while he still had his weapon would be pointless since all but Neely himself would be expendable.

Taking a shot at Neely would be suicide, not to mention foolhardy. He'd never get the shot off. Neely was too smart not to have the other lieutenants watching Court. And, Court needed him alive. Their leader was confident that these men would protect him at all cost. Court already knew that Neely liked to make a big show. He wouldn't simply shoot Court. Not enough drama. Court glanced at the tree line to his left. If he moved in that direction, he might just make it before taking a fatal hit.

But he doubted it. He would just have to figure out another scenario.

SABRINA STRAINED TO HEAR the voices outside. Even with the driver's side window open, she couldn't quite make out what was being said. She hadn't heard Court's voice, or at least she didn't think she had. She prayed he was still alive. With the windows in the car tinted so darkly, she couldn't see anything, either. If she could sit up, she might be able to see better, but each time she made even the slightest move, her guard reminded her that she'd better stay perfectly still. Sabrina glanced up at Jed Markham. He stared intently out the front windshield. She wondered if Jed realized that Joshua Neely really intended to kill her. Maybe not with his own hands, but he would order the deed done, and any one of his brainwashed soldiers would obey.

Even Jed.

Would Jed stare at her lifeless body then and realize what he had done?

Sabrina turned away, pressing her face into the sweat-smelling cloth seat. She had known Jed and his wife Amy all her life. Like the Cartwrights, they hadn't been able to have any children. And she also knew that Jed hadn't been the same since Amy died. Joshua Neely had simply come along and filled the hole left in Jed's life.

She closed her eyes and fought the sting of tears. This was real. She had dozed off sometime during the long ride. She didn't know how long ago, since, bound as she was, she couldn't look at a watch even if she'd been wearing one. Another wave of nausea washed over her and Sabrina tried to swallow, but the gag made it nearly impossible. When the car bumped over the rougher road, and then parked, Sabrina had roused from her fitful sleep. Waking up had brought the awful truth back to her—she was going to die.

Her heart ached at the thought of never seeing her baby again. Mrs. Cartwright would take good care of him, she knew. At least for as long as she was physically able. If Neely's men hadn't found Charlie, maybe even he would help with Ryan once he realized how wrong he had been. And if somehow Court had gotten away, she knew for certain that he would see after his son. He would love him as well. The hot tears leaked past her tightly closed lids. She wouldn't torture herself anymore with regret over the mistake she had made. She'd been wrong, but then, so had Court. It was too late to do anything about that now. She would spend the final minutes of her life in prayer for those she loved.

No matter what Joshua Neely did to her, she would spend the time she had left with her family fixed firmly in her mind. She would tune all of this out. Because no matter how tough life had been the past few years, she was extremely lucky to have known a man like Court and to have her son.

Her only regrets were that she wouldn't be able to raise her son and that Court would never know how much she loved him. She should have told him, but everything happened so fast and she'd been so afraid.

"Get up."

Sabrina opened her eyes at the gruff sound of Jed's voice.

"I said, get up. We got something for you to see."

As she struggled to push up into a sitting position, Sabrina thought she heard the booming voice of Joshua

Neely. Primal yells suddenly rent the air. She peered through the darkly tinted windows into the flurry of activity going on a few yards away. What had Neely said to stir such an outburst?

"Maybe this'll make you think twice about cavorting with traitors," Jed warned.

COURT WATCHED WARILY as Neely raised his hands to quiet his men's enthusiasm. He managed to ease one step closer to Neely's position while Ferguson and the others applauded until their hands surely ached. All Court needed was one or maybe two more opportunities like that and he'd be close enough to strike. It was worth a shot. He had to do something, he couldn't just stand back and wait to be eliminated.

"This is the moment we have waited for," Neely declared in that self-righteous hell-and-brimstone preacher tone he could adopt so readily.

"Our friend Mr. Fahey has performed a great service for this cause," Neely continued. "Without his offer of help we would not be here today. Nor would we be standing on the threshold of this pivotal moment. He is but one of our mighty allies. There are others who stand poised on this important precipice." He swept his arms around him in a magnanimous manner. "Soon we will have the freedom for which our forefathers fought. Our brothers in the Black Order will stand behind us, providing fortification. No longer will we lurk in the shadows, a forgotten reminder of what once was. We will step into the light and make ourselves known."

Another round of exuberant applause followed the

words Court needed to hear. Neely was working with the Black Order. Damn. Austin needed that information. Between Neely, all this firepower, and the Order, something big was going down. Court was sure of it. He gained a few more feet toward his goal. Almost there.

One of Fahey's men passed a steel case, similar to those containing the money, only more rectangular in shape, to Ferguson. *The Demo.* Cold, dark tension gripped Court's throat. This was the real killing machine. If that case contained even half as much as Court feared it did, Neely now had enough explosives to take down an area the size of a city block with the ease of leaving a thermos on a cafeteria table in the right place.

Ferguson held the case high for all to see. A roar of victory rolled over the assembled group. Desperation twisted in Court's gut. He had to do something. He couldn't let Neely leave this place with that kind of firepower.

"This *Demo*—" Neely indicated the case Ferguson so proudly held "—will enable us to do our job with the smallest possible loss of life to our number." Approval and sounds of agreement reverberated through the men. Neely nodded and Ferguson loaded the case into the jeep they had shared.

Court had been right. Neely had big plans. Court derived no pleasure from the realization.

"Mr. Fahey," Neely said, turning his attention to the man before him. "We invite you to stay a few minutes longer and enjoy a very special climax to our successful transaction this day."

Fahey glanced at his watch. "My time is limited."

"Only a few minutes," Neely insisted. "This I think you will want to see."

This was it.

Court twisted and propelled himself toward Neely, simultaneously withdrawing his Beretta. His left arm went around Neely's neck, his right hand bringing the barrel of the weapon level on the man's temple. Almost as if in slow motion, the sound of weapons engaging filled the air.

"Nobody move!" Court commanded.

"Do you really think you're going to be able to walk out of here, Court?" Neely asked.

Court backed up a couple of steps, dragging Neely with him. "Maybe, maybe not, but I'm damned well going to try."

Ferguson and three of the other lieutenants followed their every step, slowly closing in around them.

"Back off," Court warned Ferguson as he got too close. The man fell back a step. Court's heart pounded like a drum, beating out the anticipation of the next move on his left or right. Or, hell, even behind him.

Neely suddenly dug in his heels and stopped short. "Enough," he proclaimed loudly.

Court glanced at the tree line—not quite close enough to make a run for it. Or, hell, maybe he'd take his chances. "Don't make me pull this trigger," he warned Neely. "I'd hate to have to kill you."

Ignoring Court's threat, Neely commanded, "Bring out the woman."

For a moment Court couldn't comprehend what Neely

meant by that order, but then he knew. The bottom dropped out of his stomach. Oh, no. They couldn't have…

Jed Markham dragged Sabrina from the car with the darkly tinted windows and pushed her forward. He stood behind her, his gun aimed directly at her head. Her hands and feet were bound, a gag tied around her mouth. While Court watched in horror, Markham leaned down and cut her feet loose, then gave her another push toward Neely.

"Let her go." The words came from Court as he lowered his weapon in immediate surrender. "You have what you want. Let her go."

Ferguson snatched the Beretta from Court's relaxed hold, then jerked from his shoulder last night's issued rifle. Markham held Sabrina only a few feet away, close enough that Court could see the sheer terror in her eyes.

"I'm afraid it's not that simple," Neely explained. "You see, we don't abide traitors or their whores."

Court went rigid with fury. The heat of it helped melt the glacier of fear threatening to turn his insides into a solid block of ice. "She didn't do anything. And she damned sure doesn't know anything."

Neely smiled as if Court were a disobedient child. "Oh, but she does now." He gestured to Fahey, who watched with interest. "I'm sure our Mr. Fahey wants no one who can identify him left to chance."

Fahey inclined his head in acknowledgment of Neely's conclusion.

"This man—" Neely pointed an accusing finger at Court "—would ruin all that we have worked so hard to accomplish. He would deem himself more capable of judging right from wrong than we. Our struggle for freedom would end here, now, with him if he had his way. He is a traitor. He has lived among us, taken our kindness, and now he would destroy us."

Outraged grumbled through the onlookers.

Court tried to reassure Sabrina with his eyes. He wanted to hold her and tell her that everything was going to be all right…somehow, but he couldn't. She was going to die and it was his fault. She had suffered so much pain already at his hand, and now this. Court felt sick to his stomach. Why couldn't Neely just let her go?

"I say kill him," Ferguson called out above the grumblings.

"Death," another cried.

"Kill him!" yet another agreed.

Neely turned back to Court, a satisfied expression on his face. "You see, Court, my followers are faithful to me. Your short friendship, just like your life, means nothing to them. Nothing at all."

"Shoot me, then," Court demanded, "but let Sabrina go. She's innocent," he added, grinding out the words.

"By your sins, her fate has already been sealed."

Court stepped in close, getting right in Neely's face. Ferguson nudged him with his rifle, but Court ignored the warning. "I'll see you in hell, Neely, maybe not today, but soon. Very soon."

Neely smiled. "The only question now is," he began as if Court had said nothing at all, "who dies first?"

Talons of fear ripped at Court's chest. Sabrina trembled so hard she could barely stand, tears streamed down her pale cheeks. He had to do something.

"Do you have any last words, Court Brody?" Neely

asked, ever the dramatic leader. "An apology, perhaps, or maybe you would like an opportunity to plead for your life rather than toss useless threats."

"Yeah, I've got something to say," Court returned, his barely restrained fury mixed with fear for Sabrina making his voice tight. Go for broke, Brody, he told himself. *You might not have your Beretta, but you do have one thing...the truth.* He turned to the men standing in judgment of him.

"He said I was out to destroy you, but that's not true." A couple of the men voiced their opinions otherwise. Court shook his head. "I've watched you—all of you. You're good people. Do you really know the kind of man he is?" He pointed to Neely. "And him." He hitched his thumb in Fahey's direction. "Do you really want to listen to a man who does business with a terrorist organization like the Black Order? Do you have any idea the gravity of an arrangement like that?"

"Talk all you want to, Brody," Neely encouraged. "They're not going to be swayed by anything you say."

"The Black Order," Court shouted, his determination gaining momentum now, "kills innocent women and children—like yours—" Court pointed to one of the men who had brought his two boys to the compound on more than one occasion "—and yours." He gestured to another. "That case Ferguson stashed in the jeep, the Demo, it's used to blow up buildings. Buildings where people go to work, where children go to day care."

He surveyed the now completely silent group. "Like in Oklahoma City. Women and children." Court paused a moment to compose himself. He was banking on the fact that the Sons and Daughters of Montana didn't want to harm innocent people. They stood firm against those who went against their ideals, nothing more. "Is that why you're here today? To give this man—" he glared at Neely "—the power to kill innocent people?

"He won't tell you that himself, but that's exactly what he intends to do…and that's why I'm here." Court turned back to the visibly shaken men dressed in soldier garb. "I came to stop *him*…not you."

"Tell him he's wrong, Joshua," one of the men yelled.

Ferguson darted a worried glance at Neely, then back at the men.

"Tell him, Joshua, that's not what we're about," another shouted, outraged.

"I watched the news for weeks about that bombing in Oklahoma City," Raymond piped up, cutting Court a hard glare. "We ain't got nothing like that in mind." He turned his attention to Neely. "Tell him, Joshua."

Court waited, his heart hammering, for Neely to respond.

The man glowered at Court, fury blazing in his eyes. "How dare you question my ideals." He turned back to the waiting men, their faces expectant. "Surely you are not foolish enough to believe that anything can be accomplished without the spilling of some innocent blood?" he demanded, his arrogance showing. "No ground can ever be gained without grabbing the world's attention. No one has forgotten the images from Oklahoma City, just as no one will ever be able to forget what we stand for."

Expressions filled with uncertainty, the men stood

silent, waiting for Neely to continue. For him to somehow explain away his own words.

Court felt the subtle shift, felt his hopes rising. The man was digging his own damned grave. Court sent another reassuring look in Sabrina's direction. She still trembled, but the tears had dried. Court's chest constricted. If he could just have one more chance...

Neely pointed to the trucks loaded with weapons. "This is the only way," he insisted with a calm Court was sure he couldn't possibly feel. "You can be certain that I have given these details much consideration. And, in time, you will understand as I do. For now, it is imperative that we conclude this business."

"But you didn't say nothin' about killin' no women and children," Beecham, standing next to Raymond, countered.

"After our rally tonight," Neely thundered, pressing the man with an intimidating gaze, "all your questions will be answered."

Stunned silence, or maybe acquiescence, Court couldn't be sure which, was the only response.

Neely shifted a triumphant gaze to Court. "You cannot stop what has already been set in motion," he warned for Court's ears only.

"Maybe I won't have to." Court glanced at the confused men, hoping against hope that all were not fooled.

Neely smirked at Court's insinuation, "You think you can stop me so easily? No matter what happens here today, this destiny is already set. And you're already dead."

CHAPTER TWELVE

"THE WOMAN DIES first," Neely commanded.

Court readied to hurl his body in front of Sabrina's the moment he determined from which way the harm would come. She trembled, her stance so unsteady Markham held her upright.

"But she's a teacher with my wife," Beecham, the man Court had chosen as a volunteer, said. Standing right beside him, Raymond looked worried and confused.

Neely whirled toward Beecham, accusation in his eyes. "Would you choose to die in her place?" he demanded.

"She's just a teacher," another man repeated.

"The wages of disloyalty is death." Neely turned to Ferguson. "Kill them both, and anyone who takes their side."

Before the order sank into the heads of those protesting, Ferguson shot the second man who had spoken out against Neely. Before Court could reach him, Ferguson took a bead on Beecham then. Raymond dived to the right, taking the round in his right shoulder, and knocking Beecham clear of the shot. Court snagged Ferguson's arm, sending his next shot into the ground.

The sound of helicopter blades cutting through the air vibrated in the distance. Court glanced up. It had to be Daniel Austin. He prayed it was Austin. The rhythmic whoop-whoop grew louder, signaling their nearness. Then all hell broke loose.

Court lunged at Ferguson, who was struggling toward Sabrina. They went down together, Ferguson's weapon flying uselessly in another direction. Court caught him by the throat and squeezed. Ferguson fought hard, flopping like a fish, throwing Court onto his back. Court got in a punch before Ferguson could get a choke-hold on him. The blow rattled Ferguson for an instant. Court swung again, his fist connecting hard with the man's jaw. Ferguson crumpled.

Court pushed an unconscious Ferguson off him and scrambled to his feet. He had to get to Sabrina. Steadying himself, Court scanned the crazed crowd. Where the hell was she? Then he spotted her. Markham was attempting to force her into the car. Court ran like hell in that direction and propelled himself over the hood, sliding to the other side and landing right behind Markham.

Markham swung around to face Court, with Sabrina pulled against him like a shield. "Don't come near me or I'll shoot her. I swear I will!"

Court ignored all sounds, including the exchange of gunfire, and concentrated only on the man in front of him. "Jed, just calm down, buddy." Court swallowed back the fear climbing into his throat. Sabrina's face was sheet-white, her eyes wide with terror.

"I just wanna get outta here," Jed told him, his expression nearly as frightened as Sabrina's.

Court had to tread very carefully, the man was on the

edge, scared out of his mind. Confused by what he'd seen and heard. "I understand." Court eased closer. "You can go. All you have to do is drop your weapon and release Sabrina. I don't have any beef with you. Just let her go and you can leave."

Jed shook his head. He glanced at the turmoil behind Court. "I don't think so. They're killing one another over there."

The helicopter had landed, but the shots and heated shouts continued to fly behind Court. "Okay, buddy, then you take me and release Sabrina," Court offered, moving closer still.

Sabrina cried out, the gag preventing her from speaking. She shook her head adamantly in an effort to change Court's mind.

"You armed?" Jed studied Court cautiously.

Court lifted his arms above his head and turned all the way around for the man to see that he wasn't. His pulse quickened as hope flickered inside him. He had to see that Sabrina was safe.

"All right." Jed stepped around Sabrina, taking a bead on Court. "You'll do."

"Stay down, Brin," Court told her. "Stay down behind one of the vehicles until this is over."

Sobbing, she obediently sank to the ground.

Anxious, Jed glanced around. "Let's get outta here."

"Lower your weapon, Jed," Court warned, "before somebody from my team sees you and thinks you intend to kill me."

Further confused, Jed just stood there staring at him. Court took the weapon from his hand and ushered the man toward the tree line. "Go," he told him. "Get the hell out of here."

Jed blinked once, still uncertain, then he ran as fast as he could into the woods. Court hurried back to Sabrina. He pulled her to her feet and untied the gag. While he fumbled with the ropes on her hands he surveyed the turmoil only a few yards away. Austin and the ATF appeared to have the situation under control now. The Confidential crew had recognized the need for ATF backup. Good thing, Court mused. He couldn't tell anything about the casualty rate yet, but several bodies littered the ground.

"Court!" With her hands free now, Sabrina hugged him close. "I thought they killed you last night." She cried in earnest against his chest.

Court held her as tightly as he dared. "They probably would have if Neely wasn't such a pompous fool. He wanted to make a big production of it." He exhaled wearily. "Which probably saved both our lives."

He drew back from her enough to look into her eyes. "I thought I told you to hightail it on over to the Lonesome Pony."

She swiped at her damp cheeks. "I made a mistake and then Ferguson and his men came for us."

"Where's Ryan?" His heart stalled between beats.

"I hid him in the old fruit cellar with Mrs. Cartwright."

Court smiled his relief. "Good thinking." He kissed her forehead. "You did good, Brin."

She shuddered. "But Charlie slipped out of the house before they got there. I'm praying that he didn't go back to the compound."

Court thought about that for a minute. "I don't think he did. We were there until around two this morning making preparations and then we headed here. If he'd shown up I think I would have seen him."

She pushed away the strands of hair the gag had worked loose from her ponytail. "Where would he go?"

"Court, you okay?" Daniel Austin skidded to a stop next to them. His concerned gaze traveled first over Court, then over Sabrina. "We were really worried about you, buddy."

"We're fine." Court felt better knowing Austin was here. He frowned then. "What the hell are you doing here?" Coming into a situation like this was risky. Austin should have stayed clear of the danger and let the ATF handle it. They'd stayed out of the picture as long as they intended to, Court felt certain.

Austin shrugged. "I had to make sure you were okay."

So the guy cared.

"Kyle's over there with a small bomb squad unit to handle transporting the Demo," Austin went on to explain.

Court searched for Kyle in the group of militia soldiers being handcuffed and read their rights. The sandy-haired Confidential agent appeared deeply engrossed in a conversation with five other men, including Fahey. A serious expression held the place of the quick grin that usually spread so effortlessly across Kyle Foster's face. Court needed to get over there, but the thought of leaving Sabrina made him hesitate.

"What's the tally over there?"

"We've got seven dead, including Neely and Ferguson."

Startled by that announcement, Court snapped his

gaze to Austin's. "Ferguson? I knocked him cold. He shouldn't—"

"He's dead, Court," Austin repeated solemnly.

Court swore. With both Neely and Ferguson dead, that reduced the likelihood of discovering Neely's ultimate goal down to next to nothing.

Austin smiled, a weary expression. "But we got Fahey. The ATF guys are as happy as ticks on a dog."

"We needed Neely alive." Court scrubbed a hand over his face. "Neely was definitely working with the Black Order. But I don't know to what end." Court shrugged tiredly. "Hell, maybe Fahey knows something, but I doubt it. Neely liked to keep things close, then announce them with as much showy display as possible."

"I think we should call your Bureau pals at Quantico," Austin suggested, "and have them send us a special interrogator for Fahey and the surviving lieutenants." Austin scanned the arrest activities taking place around them. "If Fahey knows anything, the guys from Quantico'll get it out of him."

I think? Was Austin actually asking Court's advice? "That sounds like a good plan." The nod Court received in response told him that Austin had, in fact, wanted his input.

"Sabrina!"

Sabrina whipped around at the sound of Charlie's voice. "Charlie!" Faint with relief, she opened her arms just in time for Charlie to run into them. "God, Charlie, I was so afraid something had happened to you."

"What the hell is he doing here?" Court demanded, his arm still curled around Sabrina's back.

She was so thankful that they were all safe. Now, if she just had Ryan in her arms.

"He wouldn't have it any other way," Austin explained. "He said if we didn't bring him here he'd follow us in his old pickup truck, and trust me, that would have been even more dangerous."

Sabrina pushed Charlie back and took a good look at him just to be sure he was unharmed. "How did you know to go to Mr. Austin?"

"I heard the whole thing!" Charlie said, his eyes wide with remembered fear. "I'd just climbed out of my bedroom window when I heard somebody drive up. By the time I got around to the side of the house, Ferg was already in there with you. I could hear everything he said through the window. I'd done heard you tell Mrs. Cartwright that we'd all go to the Lonesome Pony the next morning. So I knew where to go. I couldn't let 'em hurt you." Charlie lowered his gaze. "I can't believe I trusted him."

Sabrina hugged him tight again. "It's okay. A lot of people trusted Ferguson." Pride bloomed in her chest. Charlie was a hero. But she still didn't know about her baby. "What about Ryan and Mrs. Cartwright? Are they okay?" She had to know if her baby was safe. "Did you help them out of the cellar?"

"They're at the Lonesome Pony," Austin put in quickly. "Safe and sound."

"Thank God," Court breathed the words.

Sabrina patted the hand resting on her waist and gave Court her best smile. "We're all safe." She frowned suddenly. "But how did you get to the Lonesome Pony?" she asked Charlie, the question only now filtering through her haze of relief. "Did Mrs. Cartwright drive you?"

Charlie shook his head adamantly. "Naw, she was too upset when I pulled her outta that fruit cellar. She said she shoulda stayed in her own bed."

A bark of laughter burst from Sabrina. The poor old lady. She had wanted to go home and sleep in her own bed, but Sabrina had insisted that she stay with her. "Did Mrs. Cartwright have her medicine with her?"

Charlie nodded. "And just as soon as she took it, we headed to Mr. Austin's place."

Sabrina's eyes rounded. "You drove?"

"I sure did!" He beamed a bright smile. "Got us there in one piece, too."

"Well, that's a matter of opinion, young man," Austin said skeptically. "You did clear out a fence row here and there before you got that truck parked."

Red flagged Charlie's cheeks. "I'll fix your fence for you, Mr. Austin."

Austin smiled. "You don't worry about that fence, Charlie. I'd rather you concentrate on driving lessons."

Sabrina hugged Charlie's shoulders. "You did good, Charlie boy. I knew I could count on you when the chips were down."

His gaze turned somber again. "I'm sorry about all that stuff I said," he mumbled. "I don't wanna go back to the militia compound anymore."

"Good." Sabrina blinked back the tears brimming in her eyes. It felt good to have her brother back. She hugged him until she thought her arms would fall off. "We're going to be fine, Charlie, I promise."

"Brin, I need to check on Raymond and Fahey," Court said softly. She'd forgotten he was still standing beside her. Austin had disappeared.

She nodded and offered Court a watery smile. They were safe, and right now that was all that mattered. She watched him stride across the clearing. She would deal with his decisions concerning their son later. Right now she was too physically and mentally exhausted to feel anything but relief.

"I love you, Charlie," she murmured in her brother's ear.

"I love you, sis."

Court surveyed the wounded. The paramedics appeared to be doing a pretty good job of patching up Raymond. The bullet had gone clear through, apparently not hitting anything vital.

"That was a brave thing you did, Raymond," Court told him. It was only Raymond's quick thinking that saved Beecham. "I'll make sure that's considered when they try your case."

Raymond lifted his gaze to Court's. None of the animosity or bitterness Court had fully expected was there. Only a heavy sadness.

"I didn't know it would be this way." Raymond shook his head. "I didn't know."

Court squeezed the man's good shoulder. "I know, buddy. I know."

Seven of Neely's soldiers were dead. Neely lay alongside the very man, one of his own followers, who had apparently killed him. Court shook his head at the irony of it all. How did lunatics like Neely ever make it this far? If they could figure that out maybe they could prevent days like this from happening again. Court scanned the clearing, then the wide Montana sky. Another eagle, or hell, maybe it was the same one, flew overhead, viewing the havoc left by an egomaniac and his followers.

Two AFT agents had just finished loading the last of the prisoners. Only Fahey remained, his hands secured. Court supposed the ATF wanted to transport him separately from the others. He didn't blame them. The capture of the infamous Fahey was a major coup.

"I thought you were a dead man, Brody," Fahey remarked as Court walked past him.

One corner of Court's mouth lifted in a gesture that felt more like a grimace than a smile. "Guess I'm just lucky."

"Maybe next time," Fahey suggested when Court would have walked away.

Court turned back to look at him. "Maybe, but one thing's certain, you definitely won't be there to see it."

Fahey inclined his head, yielding the point and match to Court. "Those men—" Fahey gestured to the militia soldiers being driven away in the two ATF vans "—the biggest part of them had no intention of allowing Neely to kill you."

"Really, and how did you arrive at that conclusion?" Court watched him closely, looking for any subtle mannerism that might give away his deceit.

"I did what you're doing now," Fahey said with a smile. "I watched them. Most of them were shocked by the unveiling of who Neely really was. I had a front-row seat, remember?" he added when Court looked skeptical.

"Maybe," Court relented.

"No maybes," Fahey countered as he studied the cuffs on his wrists. "The ones I watched really liked you, considered you one of them. Maybe it's because just like them, this is your home."

Court started, just a little, at that remark. "This isn't home," he denied, summoning his condo to mind.

Fahey shrugged. "Whatever. I know what I saw."

"You just keep telling us what you know," Court told him bluntly, "and maybe they'll go easy on you."

After checking on Sabrina and Charlie, Court strode to the communications van to talk to Austin. Something Neely said was nagging at him.

When Austin had finished his cellular call, Court ushered him away from the other men. "Look, there may still be something going down."

"What do you mean?" Austin's face was a study in concentration.

"It may be nothing, but right before all hell broke loose around here, Neely said something to me that has me a little worried."

"Go on."

"He said something like you can't stop what's already set in motion." Court considered those tense moments again, remembering each word. *"No matter what happens here today, this destiny is already set."*

Austin rubbed his chin. "Anything else?"

Frowning, Court shook his head. "No. Just that. But it sounded like a warning or a threat. And we know now that he was definitely working with the Black Order." Court took a deep breath and let it out slowly. "It's more than just what he said. Something bothers me about the way he said the words. It was a promise. Almost like he was trying to be prophetic."

"The forensics team is coming in this afternoon. They're going to take apart Neely's office and his command center. If he was hiding anything, they'll find it. And if Fahey knows anything we'll get that as well." Austin clapped Court on the back. "You've had a rough day, buddy. Take Sabrina and Charlie home. You can come by the ranch tomorrow around noon and we'll talk some more. I think Frank and C.J. have a big backyard bash planned to celebrate their one-month anniversary or something foolish like that."

Marriage. To Court's surprise he didn't flinch at the thought. Nor did the typical antirelationship notions flood his brain. Should he consider that a bad sign? No, he should do exactly like Austin told him. He should take Sabrina and Charlie home, get some rest, and try to figure out all these other jumbled-up problems later.

He had a son.

His gaze instantly sought Sabrina. He had a woman who cared deeply for him.

Now all he had to do was decide what to do about it.

Only a few thousand miles stood between them.

Court walked slowly back to where Charlie and Sabrina stood watching the strangely organized frenzy of activity. It was always that way at the scene of a bust, especially when one went a little south and a whole lot east. He and Sabrina had barely escaped with their lives. One small shift either way and they could both be dead now and being loaded into body bags instead of those men on the ground.

Fate had given them another chance. Or maybe it was

simply their destiny to be together. Court's brows furrowed. The word *destiny* made him think about Neely's warning. He knew it meant something. He just knew it. He'd have to convince Austin somehow.

"We can leave now," Court told Sabrina. She looked beyond exhausted. He had to get her home. It was a long drive. Maybe she could get some rest on the way.

"Good." Sabrina rubbed her eyes. "I'm definitely ready to put this behind me and get home to my son."

Our son. Court didn't correct her. He pushed thoughts of Ryan away for the moment. They were both too tired to talk about it. "You ready, Charlie?"

The kid nodded. "Can I drive?"

Court's mouth kicked up into a one-sided grin. "I don't think so." He ruffled the kid's hair. "Maybe another time. Okay?"

"I just need some practice, that's all."

"That's what I hear." Court ushered them toward a jeep. He felt reasonably sure that Sabrina would not want to ride in the car again, considering she'd been held prisoner in it.

Charlie climbed into the back. "Man, I'd love to have one of these."

Court helped Sabrina into her seat, then skirted the hood and swung in behind the wheel. "Maybe I'll let you drive it before we turn it in to the ATF. They'll confiscate all these vehicles."

"Cool!" Charlie fastened his seat belt and lounged back on his seat as if he were in hog heaven.

"Try to get some sleep." Court reached for his own seat belt. "It's a long drive."

"Brody!"

Court looked in the direction of the man who'd shouted his name. One of the ATF guys, followed by Kyle Foster, hurried toward the jeep.

"I'm Special Agent in Charge O'Conner," the man explained. "I think you already know Agent Kyle Foster."

Court nodded, his gaze lingering on Foster a moment. Something was very wrong. Court could see it in Foster's eyes, in the drawn expression on his face. The man was pale, like he felt sick to his stomach. Like he didn't need to be here.

Hell, did any of them really want to be here?

"What's up?" Court ventured, uneasiness spreading through him like fire catching in dead grass.

"Can we speak privately?" O'Conner glanced at Sabrina and Charlie, then settled his gaze back on Court's.

"Sure." Court reassured Sabrina with a quick smile. "Be right back." He undid his seat belt and pushed out of the jeep. What the hell was up now?

"Where did Neely put the Demo?" O'Conner looked more than a little rattled at the moment.

Court looked from O'Conner to Foster, then gestured to the jeep Neely and Ferguson had arrived in. "Behind the seat. Ferguson stored it there as soon as he got through showing it off." A couple of guys, from the bomb squad, Court presumed, were inspecting the jeep in question.

Foster shook his head. "It's not there. No case, no nothing. Are you sure that's where he put it?"

Court stilled. "It has to be. I saw him put it there."

O'Conner shook his head. "It's simply not there."

It had to be there. Court would have sworn, hotly and profusely, but for the space of two heartbeats he couldn't form any words.

"You're positive about what you saw?" Foster pressed, his voice strained.

"Positive."

"Okay, men," O'Conner shouted to his troops. "Search every vehicle again. And then again after that. If you don't find the case, then set me up a perimeter. I want every square foot of the woods immediately surrounding this clearing searched even if it takes all day and all night."

"Better put in a call and have the prisoners questioned as soon as they arrive at the holding unit," Court suggested, his mind reeling with possibilities. How had someone disappeared with that case without being seen? "We need a precise head count." Twenty-four men, including Court but not counting Neely, had arrived at this location. Fahey and six of his men. That made thirty-two men. The only one missing that Court was aware of was Markham. And Court knew he didn't take the case.

"We're looking for thirty bodies and/or men besides me," Court told O'Conner. "If anyone is unaccounted for, we need to know who it is, fast. A guy named Markham took off right after the shooting started but he was unarmed and empty-handed."

O'Conner was already calling in the request. They would soon know if anyone had slipped through their fingers. A cold sweat slicked Court's skin. They had to find those damned explosives. If anyone got his hands on that case…it could be bad. Very, very bad.

"We'll find it," Foster offered, as if reading Court's mind. But Foster didn't look convinced at all, and he sure as hell didn't sound that way.

"I hope to God you're right," Court said tiredly.

"Counting the body bags, we got twenty-nine," O'Conner told him when he disconnected.

Court did swear this time. They had a walking time bomb on their hands. "We've got a broken-arrow situation. You'd better widen that perimeter, O'Conner. If we lose that stuff—"

"I know." A line of sweat had formed on the man's upper lip. "We're screwed."

Court forced his respiration to slow in an effort to head off the renewed tension mounting inside him. "You can bet your life somebody will be."

Austin looked up from the communications van where he was using the radio again. Their gazes locked.

You cannot stop what has already been set in motion. No matter what happens here today, this destiny is already set.

Neely might be dead, but his plans were obviously alive. And carrying enough explosives to do a lot of damage.

CHAPTER THIRTEEN

COURT WATCHED THE crimson sunset alone from the front porch steps of the Double K. Mental and physical exhaustion had claimed him hours ago, but he refused to give in and close his eyes. He would not rest until this was over.

He couldn't.

They had looked for hours without finding the Demo. Court had known they wouldn't find it. Greg Potts, the only lieutenant unaccounted for, had obviously taken it and fled the scene at the first sign of trouble. Just as he had, no doubt, been instructed. Court remembered Potts from his first visit to the hole. Potts had been the one to come forward and embrace him before anyone else. *Brother,* he'd said. Austin was running a check on the guy now. Kyle Foster, Montana Confidential's own bomb specialist and chemistry whiz, was tracking down every high-level scumbag he knew in the business to see if there was any word on the street as to what Neely might have been conspiring to do.

No matter what happens here today, this destiny is already set.

It was a threat, pure and simple. Court felt it all the way to his bones.

And they had nothing. The source who'd dropped the

dime on Court and blown his cover was still a complete mystery. No one from the Sons and Daughters of Montana knew anything. None of the other lieutenants would confess to any knowledge whatsoever of the plans for the explosives or Neely's higher contacts. And Court was pretty sure they didn't know anything. Raymond had come completely clean and he didn't have a clue. But the sick feeling in Court's gut wouldn't go away. Neely was just the type who would keep his ultimate plans close. Only one or two would be privy. And Ferguson, the low-life SOB, was deader than a doornail.

Just Court's luck. He'd sent Sabrina and Charlie home this morning, but he'd refused to leave the scene until he'd helped search for hours. Then Daniel Austin had ordered him to go home. Court decided he must have looked like death warmed over, for Austin hadn't allowed him to drive, he'd insisted that Court ride in one of the helicopters. *Your job is finished, Austin had said. Go home and get some rest.*

Home? Where the hell was home? Court stood. His body ached in too many places to ignore. He and Ferguson had rolled around for a couple of minutes before Court had knocked him cold. Court had needed to get to Sabrina, to make sure she was safe. After Court had left Ferguson, someone had put a bullet in the man's head, right between the eyes. To keep him from talking? Probably, Court decided. Potts, most likely. There had been too much confusion. Some of Neely's own men going after Neely, others going after Fahey and his men, Court trying to calm Markham down, and the feds closing in on the whole cluster. Court swore. He hoped the forensics team found something at the compound that would indicate what Neely might have been up to, but he had a feeling they wouldn't. Neely was too clever…too wily….

And Court felt more tired than he ever had in his entire life. He surveyed the green pastures before him, then moved down the steps to view the rest of the ranch. His attention paused on the barn he'd helped keep in shape as a kid. As Court was the youngest, the crappiest job had gotten passed down to him—mucking out stalls. Each of his brothers had done it, then passed it on. He'd tried to hate it, told his father that he did. But the truth was Court liked being close to the horses. He loved the animals. He missed working with them when he was in D.C. His friend Elmo Cornelius understood that about Court, leaving him an open invitation to come to the Virginia countryside for the weekend anytime. He could ride to his heart's desire, even muck out stalls if he wanted to. Court laughed at the memory of Elmo saying those very words to him.

A long, heavy breath sighed from Court as his gaze landed upon the house he'd lived in for most of his life. He blinked, uncertain about the feelings that welled inside him. Before he realized he'd moved, his feet had already taken him half the distance to the springhouse. He crossed the bridge that spanned the trickling stream. When the rains came, it could froth and flow like a river. But now, in the heat of late summer, a trickle was all it managed. The long shadows from the setting sun masked the usually gleaming bed of smooth rocks that had been one of his passions as a boy. He wondered if

Charlie ever waded around in that stream looking for just the right rock for his collection.

Court hesitated before stepping up onto the wooden porch. He plowed his fingers through his hair, frowning at the realization that he'd left his hat in Sabrina's house. She had offered to let him hold Ryan while she took a shower. His body still aching for her, Court had felt torn between joining her in the shower and holding his son. Ryan had won out. Court remembered tossing his hat aside and pulling the kid into his arms. There was simply no way to describe the rush he felt holding his child. It was like nothing else he had ever experienced. He wanted to protect him, to give him anything…everything.

Had his father ever felt that way, even once? Court rubbed the back of his neck. God, he was tired. That was the only time he ever let the past slip into conscious thought. He closed his eyes and allowed the images to fill his head. He could remember a time when his father had seemed to love him. But by the time Court was twelve the drinking was worse. He couldn't bring friends home for fear of his dad's behavior. Not that he got rowdy or anything, but he just acted stupid when he'd had too much of the booze. Court rarely drank for that very reason, and then only a beer or two. He would never be like his father.

At least not in that respect. Court trudged across the porch and tried the door. It was unlocked. He pushed open the door and automatically reached for the light switch. To his amazement, a dim light blinked on overhead. Why did Sabrina keep the power turned on out here? Hell, for that matter, why didn't she rent the place? At least it would generate some income.

The thought that Sabrina suffered, financially or otherwise, tore at his heart. She could have asked him for help. Court sagged against the door frame. No, she couldn't. She'd been afraid to tell him about Ryan. Because Court was a fool. Because he'd used her and left her behind without ever calling or even writing. He'd run hard and fast, hoping to put his past behind him. Wanting to forget how he'd lain in bed at night and wished he were anywhere but here. But he never could completely push this part of his life away.

Sabrina stayed with him. No matter where he was or what he was doing, she was there, in the back of his mind. Always. She owned a big piece of his heart and he hadn't wanted to admit that. He'd wanted something else, somewhere else. Anywhere but here. He was a selfish bastard.

No wonder Sabrina hadn't trusted him enough to tell him about Ryan.

He'd gotten what he deserved.

And, damn, it felt lousy.

The next question that loomed large in his mind stopped him cold. What the hell was he going to do about it?

FROM THE KITCHEN WINDOW Sabrina watched Court walk into the springhouse. She wondered if he was thinking about the past and how unhappy he'd been there. "Of course, that's what he'd be doing," she told herself impatiently.

Turning away from the window, she peeked in the oven to check the casserole she'd hastily thrown together. It wasn't anything fancy, only chicken and vegetables with a store-bought piecrust, but it would fill their empty bellies. Complaining that he couldn't wait for anything to cook, Charlie had made himself a bowl of cereal and plopped down in front of the television. Ryan was asleep in his crib. She had called to check on Mrs. Cartwright. Thankfully the sweet but forgetful old lady had charged her telephone and it was back in working order. Sabrina didn't like the thought of her at home alone without a working telephone.

Sabrina felt immensely better after a long, hot shower. She wasn't as tired as she would have been had she not slept most of the trip home. The nice ATF agent had insisted she and Charlie should get some sleep. She'd been certain she wouldn't be able to, but the long journey and gentle rocking of the vehicle had eventually lulled her to sleep despite having a stranger at the wheel. She was pretty sure Charlie had slept as well. Her gaze moved back to the window and the log house that lay beyond the spring. Court hadn't slept at all. He'd stayed behind and searched for the explosives. And since finally arriving here, he'd been…restless. Other than the time he'd spent with Ryan, Court hadn't sat still.

He wanted to leave…probably. The realization sat like a stone in her heart. She'd heard Austin tell him that his job was finished here. Was he so anxious to flee Montana already? Surely he wouldn't turn his back on Ryan so easily.

They had to talk. Sabrina checked the timer on the oven once more and headed toward her bedroom to check on Ryan. There was no time like the present to clear the air. No point in dragging out the inevitable. If he wanted to leave, she would just give Court her blessing. He didn't have to feel obligated to either her or Ryan. She smiled down at her sleeping child. Her heart overflowed with emotion at just the sight of him.

I want my son in my life. Court's words echoed through her. Did he still feel that way now that he'd had a chance to think about the overwhelming responsibility of being a father? Court resented his own father so much, did he fear being one himself? There was only one way to find out. She would simply ask him, she decided as she slipped from the room. And there was no time like the present.

"Charlie, would you turn that down a little and keep an eye on Ryan for me?" Sabrina paused in the middle of the living room, waiting for Charlie to unglue his gaze from the television set and notice that she'd spoken.

"Huh?" He looked at her and blinked, confused.

"Ryan's asleep, but I want you to keep an eye on him for me. I have to go down to the springhouse and talk to Court. Okay?"

"Yeah, sure." Charlie turned down the volume a couple of notches. "Supper ready?" he asked, his gaze once more firmly attached to the ball players on the screen.

"Not for a while yet." She smiled. It was good to have Charlie home and acting like his old self. "The timer's on. If I'm not back when it goes off, just turn the oven off, would you?"

Charlie nodded. "Tell Court he's missing a mighty good game."

"I'll tell him."

Halfway to the springhouse, Sabrina almost lost her

nerve. A long time ago, she had watched Court's window from hers on so many nights, hoping for a glimpse of him. Had he ever watched for her?

She doubted it. Well, maybe he had. There had been something between them, she was certain of that. There was something there now, something more than Ryan, but would it be enough to make him stay? She shook off the worrisome thoughts. She would know soon enough. All she had to do was ask. Court wouldn't lie to her. She looked down at herself and the old cotton, buttoned-up dress she wore. Could a man like Court really want her the way she wanted him? She wasn't really that pretty. Her breasts were too small, her legs too long. She was too skinny. Sabrina shook off her foolish thoughts. Whatever Court thought, she would soon know.

When she stepped up onto the porch, the memory of how close they'd both come to dying this very morning slowed her. Ryan and Charlie could have been left all alone. The thought of watching Court die ripped her heart in two. Neely had fully intended to kill both of them. Sabrina closed her eyes. Only Court's quick thinking had saved them. If he hadn't made the men from the militia, or at least some of them, think about what they were doing, things might have gone a whole different route.

There was no "might have" to it. Help had not arrived quite quickly enough. Court was the one who saved them. She owed him her life. She owed him Charlie's life. And she wouldn't have Ryan if it weren't for Court. She owed him everything. She loved him. She wanted him to stay. But would any of that be enough?

You can't hold him, child, unless he wants to be held.

Mrs. Cartwright's words filtered through her mind. Her elderly friend was right. Court might not want to be held on to. *By Sabrina,* anyway.

He could have someone back in D.C. That idea shook Sabrina to the core of her soul. Could he be involved with someone else and still make love to her the way he had the other morning? Surely not. Sabrina cursed herself. Just because their lovemaking had touched her so deeply, didn't mean it had him. Oh, she had no doubt that he cared about her, in some way, but his feelings might not come anywhere close to the depth of hers for him.

"Stop stalling, Korbett," Sabrina scolded. "Get it over with."

Sabrina crossed the porch, opened the door and stepped inside. She wrinkled her nose. The place smelled a little musty. She should raise the windows. She blinked, staring at the light for a second before she looked away. She'd forgotten the electricity was still on here. She remembered then that the insurance agency required the power remain on, even if everything inside was turned off and no one lived in the place. Policy rules. Dust had settled heavily onto the sparse furnishings. She'd been too tied down since Ryan had been born to take care of a second house. Always before she'd kept the place in shape.

But things were different now.

Sabrina strolled through each room downstairs, but found no sign of Court. She paused at the bottom of the stairs. He was probably in his old room.

Summoning her courage, Sabrina climbed the stairs

and took a left. Sure enough, she found Court right where she suspected he'd be…in his room. He stood on the opposite side, staring out the window he'd opened. He hadn't turned on the overhead fixture, but the light from the fading day silhouetted him.

"Did you know that I used to watch your bedroom window at night, hoping I'd get a look at you in something besides jeans and a T-shirt?"

Sabrina drew up short just inside the door. His admission startled her. "No," she replied. "I didn't."

"Well, I did." His voice was like soft velvet, floating across the room and wrapping around her, making her skin tingle from head to toe.

"And did you?" she asked, her nerves jangling. "Get what you wanted, that is?"

"Oh, yeah. Several times."

His breathy words made her tremble with anticipation. She glanced nervously around the room. The bed was long since gone, sold to a neighbor whose son had outgrown his child-size one. The dresser and bureau remained, dust-laden, in the exact spots they'd sat all those years ago.

"Were you disappointed?" The question slipped out before she could stop it.

"No."

He turned around, the smile on his face devastating to her heart. "You were gorgeous. You made my heart race like a wild mustang afraid of being captured."

She clasped her hands behind her back to keep from fidgeting. "Well, you weren't so bad yourself," she confessed. She looked away from the heat she saw in his intense gaze, feigning preoccupation with the meager furnishings.

He moved toward her. Her heart jumped. "Are you saying that you used to watch me, too?"

She strolled over to the dresser and made a face at the dusty surface. "I might have." She glanced up and caught him watching her in the mirror. "On occasion." Her cheeks flushed with the heat rushing through her. Had she just admitted that little secret out loud?

He stepped closer. She watched his approach in the mirror, her heart thumping hard against her rib cage.

"And did you like what you saw?" he demanded, his tone low, husky, filled with a sexual undercurrent that made her shiver in spite of the warm temperature of the room.

Another step disappeared between them before she found her voice.

"Mostly." She licked her lips, her throat incredibly dry.

"Mostly?" He moved in close behind her now. "What was it you liked, Brin?" He braced his hands on the dresser on either side of her and leaned in so close she could feel his warm breath against her ear.

She shrugged, embarrassed. How could she tell him that she'd loved every part of his lean young body?

He tugged at her braid, pulling free the rubber band she'd used to secure it. Her breath caught when his fingers threaded through her hair and loosened it. His gaze on hers in the mirror, he pulled her head back and whispered in her ear, "You can tell me all your secrets, Brin." His tongue darted out and traced the shell of her ear. She shivered. "And I'll tell you mine," he murmured.

"We need to talk, Court," she said, her voice wobbly.

He drew back, looking at her in the mirror, those silvery eyes flashing with the same fever she felt. "We do." He reached in front of her and started to unbutton her dress. "But first there's something I need to show you." His fingers stilled on the third button, his gaze suddenly uncertain. "If you'll let me."

The blood roaring in her ears, she nodded, too afraid to speak. She couldn't risk breaking this beautiful spell.

One by one he released each button, until her outdated dress fell open. He slipped it off her shoulders and let it puddle around her ankles. He kissed her bared shoulder, his strong fingers gripping her upper arms as if it took all his restraint to kiss her so gently.

"You're beautiful, Brin." He brushed her hair aside and kissed her neck. "So beautiful." His hands moved to her breasts, kneading, massaging, sending desire straight to her center. He rolled her nipples between his thumbs and forefingers and she gasped.

He smiled, still watching. And she watched, the visual image adding to her pleasure. He trailed a path of kisses down her back, until he was on his knees. He slowly lowered her panties. She lifted first one foot then the other for him to remove them. He pushed her dress, panties and sandals away with one sweep of his hand before he stood. His chin came to rest on her right shoulder so that he could look his fill at her in the mirror.

Sabrina's cheeks flushed at the sight of her naked body visible in the mirror. His palm flattened on her stomach, making her skin tingle there as he pressed her against him, allowing her to feel the hardness of his own arousal against her buttocks. Heat seared her at the feel of him. She closed her eyes and dropped her head back on his broad shoulder. It felt so good to be held by him.

"You're the most beautiful woman I've ever known," he murmured, kissing her cheek, her closed lids.

"Don't lie to me, Court," she protested, her voice as husky as his.

He captured her chin and forced her to look in the mirror once more. "Look at yourself, Brin. You are beautiful." He released her chin and trailed his fingers down the center of her body until he touched her *there*. "You're perfect and no matter where I went or what I did, I could never completely put you out of my head."

He parted her…slipped one long finger inside her. With his other arm he encircled her waist, holding her firmly against him. "I tried." He massaged the tiny nub swelling with desire for him and she had to bite her lower lip to keep from crying his name. "And I tried some more." He nibbled on her neck, his eyes still watching every nuance of her response to his touch. "But nothing worked."

"But you didn't come back," she argued, her voice strained with the wild pleasure mushrooming inside her.

"I was a fool," he murmured against her jaw. "I hurt you because I couldn't deal with the past. I couldn't reconcile what I had been with what I wanted to be— the polar opposite of my father."

His long finger moved deep inside her, his palm pressing so hard against her, she couldn't catch her breath for a moment. In and out, he drew on that well of desire at the very farthest reaches of her soul. "Court," she gasped. "You're driving me crazy. I can't think."

"Don't think," he said harshly, his own need obviously spiraling out of control. "Just feel, and listen."

"I was wrong." He squeezed her breast, tugged at her nipple, all the while keeping up the rhythm that was sending her headlong toward climax. "I was running just like my father, only in a different way. I know that now." He groaned, his eyes closing briefly, when she instinctively pressed her bottom more firmly against him.

"Court, please," she begged. She wanted him to take her. No more talking.

The fire in his eyes when he opened them once more made her heart skip a couple of beats. "I'm not running anymore," he growled savagely.

"Court, I…" Her eyes closed, lights pulsed there.

He stroked her harder still.

She shattered.

Sabrina moaned long and loud as the waves crashed over her again and again. She was vaguely aware that his hands were no longer working their magic. She felt him wrench his jeans open, felt his hard arousal brush against her bottom. A gasp tore from her throat at the silky feel of him.

Her feminine muscles constricted instinctively, anticipating his penetration. He pulled her bottom firmly against him as he bent his knees just enough to align his tip with the swollen flesh still throbbing from his touch. And then he filled her. The sound of ecstasy was long and low and drained all energy from her, making her sag in his hold. He rocked against her, withdrew slightly, then pushed deep again, stretching her. She called his name, straightened, reaching for him, burying her fingers deep in his thick hair. His left hand flattened against her abdomen, holding her in place, while his right slid down to the place so tight with him. He teased that throbbing nub, doubling the sensations raging along her nerve endings.

His breath was ragged in her ear, his body so hard she could feel each and every muscle defined against hers. A ripple of pure delight triggered her spasms all over again. She made a sound, almost a shriek. Court reacted, pumping harder, groaning savagely. She forced her eyes open to watch. She wanted to see his face when he reached his own release. To see the truth of his words. Desire shuddered through her when her gaze collided with his. He was watching, his expression so intent her heart squeezed painfully. His fingers dug into her flesh as he thrust into his own climax. Sensations rained down on Sabrina as she went over the edge. He slowed, pouring the last of his scorching release into her. And then he trembled. His arms went tight around her, holding her closer to him, while he remained ensheathed deep within her.

Attempting to catch her breath, she could only stare at the big strong man who looked so suddenly vulnerable. So completely lost to what they had just shared.

"I love you, Brin," he murmured. "I hope you can forgive me."

CHAPTER FOURTEEN

"YOU'RE SURE ABOUT this," Sabrina asked Court for the third time the next morning.

With Ryan held high above his head, Court made exaggerated faces and sounds for his small but captive audience. Sabrina's heart leapt with emotion at the sight of father and son so engrossed in each other. Ryan snagged Court's nose, cooing and squealing with delight.

Court pulled his son close to his chest and kissed him on his silky head. "I'm positive, Brin," he assured her. "What do I have to do to convince you that I'm serious?"

Heat flooded her body at the memory of the way he had shown her in no uncertain terms how much he wanted her again last night well after Charlie had gone upstairs to bed. Court had spent the night in her bed, his arms around her. But he'd kissed her and slipped away for a few hours at dawn. He hadn't told her where he'd gone or what he'd been doing when he returned around ten this morning. In a way, she supposed, it had been for the best. Charlie was at an impressionable age, and Sabrina didn't want to do anything that might confuse him or make him feel uncomfortable. He'd been through enough with Neely.

She was well aware that Court was serious about

leaving the Bureau. She'd seen the truth in his eyes last night. He loved her. He loved their son. He wanted to stay. But would he be happy as the months and years went by? Or would his heart grow restless again when he'd been here for a while?

"I love you, Brin." Court pulled her close and kissed her forehead. "I'm through running from my past. I have a special assignment now—my son. Here, take Ryan. I have something for you."

Sabrina cuddled her baby in her arms, cherishing his sweet baby smell.

"Sit," Court ordered, gesturing to the couch.

Obeying, she settled onto the edge of the cushion and put Ryan down on the floor. Grinning, he held on to her knee and started his little bouncing dance. She wiped his chin with his bib and tweaked his cute little button nose. He gurgled his approval and waved his free arm.

Court knelt on one knee next to their son. Sabrina smiled at him, thinking that he intended to play with Ryan some more, but Court's gaze remained fixed on her. Worry drew her lips into a frown. "Is something wrong?"

He produced and opened a small velvet box. Inside was the most beautiful ring she had ever seen. Her heart galloped, then nearly bucked to a stop. So this explained his little disappearing act this morning. Fierce emotion made speech impossible. She searched his gaze, afraid to believe, more afraid not to.

"Sabrina, I'd like you to marry me," he said, his eyes relaying the sincerity of his words.

Before she could respond, Ryan reached up and grabbed Court's ear.

Court pulled Ryan onto his knee. "That is," he amended, "if it's okay with our boy."

"What if the Bureau tries to change your mind?" Sabrina persisted. "You do love your job."

Court dipped his head in acknowledgment. "I do. But I talked to Daniel Austin this morning and he's asked me to stay on here if I want." Court shrugged. "I think I'll eventually fit in. Austin said that Raymond has volunteered to work with us in an effort to diffuse more groups like Neely's in exchange for probation. I'd like that opportunity. I don't want what happened here to happen again someplace else. Men like Neely are dangerous."

"So you'd work for Austin?" she ventured hesitantly.

"When he needs me, but mostly I'd be busy getting this ranch going again. And taking care of my family." He took her hand in his. "We can do it, Brin, I know we can. Please say yes."

She covered her mouth with her free hand to hold back the sob rising in her throat. She ordered the tears to retreat. She would not cry and ruin Court's perfect proposal. After clearing her throat to steady her voice, she looked deeply into his eyes and said "Yes," with all her heart.

A FEW MINUTES BEFORE noon Court maneuvered the car through the turnoff that led to the Lonesome Pony ranch. He reached over to ruffle Charlie's hair. "That's some trail you cut in that ditch," he teased.

"Hey," Charlie shot back, "I got us here."

From the back seat of Mrs. Cartwright's car, Sabrina laughed. Ryan cooed from his car seat as if he'd understood the joke as well.

"I wish Mrs. Cartwright would have come with us," Sabrina said wistfully. "I hate that she spends so much time alone."

Court glanced at Sabrina in the rearview mirror. "Ah, I don't think she's going to be alone today," he said slowly.

"Really?" Sabrina looked puzzled.

Court parked the car. "She said something about a Mr. Ledbetter coming by later for lunch."

Sabrina's eyes widened. "You're kidding? That old man has been after her for years. I can't believe she's finally changing her tune."

Court quickly got out and opened the back door to take Ryan from his car seat. "Well, maybe that little scare in the fruit cellar made her decide to grab all the gusto she could get before it's too late." Court winked. "You think?"

Sabrina smiled back at him. "Maybe." She picked up Ryan's diaper bag. "Whatever the case, I'm happy for her."

"I'll see y'all later." Charlie slammed his door and dashed off.

Court squinted after him. Where the heck was he going in such an all-fired hurry? In the distance, apparently waiting for Charlie, Court could just make out another figure. A girl? Jewel? The McMurtys' grand-daughter. Court didn't know they knew each other. Maybe they'd seen each other in school.

With his son in his arms and the woman he loved at his side, Court led the way to the back of the house. He could smell the food grilling. For the first time in too long to remember he felt completely relaxed. Even

Neely's final remarks to him had stopped nagging him—at least it had since Court had spent last night with Sabrina. All other thought had ceased.

He looked from his son to Sabrina and then to the gang gathered around the grill in the backyard, and Court suddenly realized just how much his life had changed in the past few days. He had gone from single-mindedness about his job to being a father, an almost husband and a new member of the Confidential team. A real member, he hoped. Court still wasn't sure he had gained Frank and Kyle's respect. Austin was a different story. Court smiled at the typical American setting before him. He and Austin understood each other, professionally speaking.

"Court! Sabrina!" C.J. called out when she looked up from the grill.

Court had a feeling that she was supervising Frank's work. Kyle was busy with his daughter, Molly. And Austin, well he was kicked back in a lounge chair, watching the fun. Judging from C.J.'s exuberant greeting, Austin had already filled the crew in on Sabrina.

Whitney waved a welcome, her cell phone attached to her ear as usual.

Smiling widely, Austin pushed to his feet. "Glad you folks could make it." He gave Sabrina a peck on the cheek, then turned to Court. "Good news," he told him. "O'Conner picked up Potts about half an hour ago."

Court's pulse kicked up. "The Demo?"

A broad smile slid across Austin's face. "Got it."

Profound relief rushed through Court. It was over. Whatever Neely's plan, it would never see fruition. "Thank God," Court breathed.

"And who's this young fella?" Austin tugged on Ryan's bib.

"This is my son, Ryan," Court said without hesitation.

A moment of awkward silence followed as all eyes shifted to Court. "And this is my fiancée, Sabrina Korbett," he added before anyone found their tongues. Apparently Austin hadn't mentioned Ryan. He'd left that announcement to Court.

Within seconds, Sabrina was surrounded by the women. Whitney, C.J., even Dale McMurty, admired her engagement ring. Sabrina literally beamed. The vision took Court's breath. She had waited two years too long for this moment. He wanted her to enjoy it now.

"Whitney, you owe me fifty bucks," Kyle shouted over the hubbub.

Her only response was a feigned smile.

"Why does she owe you fifty bucks?" Court shifted Ryan to the other arm.

"Remember—" C.J. answered for Kyle in her elegant accent "—I told you the two of them were laying wagers on who would walk down the aisle next."

And Court remembered very well his unspoken reply. He was never going to get married. He'd even felt sorry for Foster and his motherless little girl. Court kissed his son's chubby cheek. Well, that was before. He had all the reason in the world to get married now. Court felt a tug on his pants leg. He looked down to find the little girl in question, Molly, staring up at him.

"Is that your baby?" she asked, her green eyes wide with curiosity. "Or did you b'ar him from s'mbody?"

Court crouched down to her level. "He's mine. Would you like to play with him? His name is Ryan."

She nodded enthusiastically, blond curls bouncing. Court settled Ryan on his feet and allowed Molly to take his hand.

"C'mon, Ryan, I gotta dolly ov'r here." The little girl led Ryan slowly to the blanket where her toys were spread out.

Court did a quick visual survey for anything Ryan shouldn't play with. He'd heard Sabrina fuss at Charlie this morning for leaving change and some sort of electronic game gadget on the coffee table.

Frank left his cooking duties in C.J.'s capable hands and walked straight up to Court and clapped him on the back. "We're glad to have you on board, Brody. You did a good job on this assignment."

Neely's words nagged at Court again. He shook his head. He couldn't believe it was really over. But it was. They'd found Potts and the explosives. Yet, it still sounded too good to be true. "I kept waiting for the other shoe to drop," he told Frank. "I had a bad feeling that Neely wasn't finished." But he was, Court reminded himself. Neely was dead, and whatever plans he'd had died with him.

Frank smiled. "Neely's history, and so is that assignment. Give it a rest, man."

Court had never seen the man smile before. Maybe there were some people who marriage really did agree with. And Frank was right, Court had done his job. He had to put it behind him now. Neely was gone. He had a whole new future to look forward to. His gaze drifted to Sabrina as she lifted their son into her arms. The kind of future he'd only just realized was the one he'd wanted all along.

The sound of a vehicle approaching jerked Court from his intense reverie. A delivery van from a floral shop in Livingston braked to a stop at the side of the house. Mrs. McMurty pulled free from the women's circle and headed over to greet the driver.

"I figured that would be UPS," Kyle said with a laugh. "I swear Whitney gets a delivery almost every day. The woman is a shopping maniac."

"Whitney has her finer points," C.J. offered in defense of her friend. "She's had a tough time of it adjusting to the 'wilderness,' as she would put it."

Kyle looked instantly contrite. "Just running off at the mouth," he said by way of apology.

Court remembered that there'd been some sort of stink between Ross Weston, one of Montana's esteemed senators, and Whitney, and she'd wound up exiled to this "wilderness."

Sabrina stepped up and wrapped her arm around Court's making him forget all about senators or crazy militia leaders. "Hi," he murmured.

"Thanks for bringing us," she murmured back.

"We're a team now," Court assured her. "Together."

She smiled, and Court melted. God, how he loved this woman.

Mrs. McMurty strutted in their direction, carrying a huge bouquet of roses and an envelope. "They're for you, dear," she said to Whitney.

"For me?" Whitney looked totally confused.

"That's what the card says," the older woman insisted.

Whitney accepted the flowers and sat them on the garden table. She glanced at the card, then tore open the envelope while the other women carried on about how beautiful the roses were and how lucky Whitney was to have such a generous admirer. Court decided he had to order some flowers like that for Sabrina. In fact, there were a lot of things he intended to do for his future wife. He had money. Hell, he'd saved nearly half of everything he'd ever earned, and he'd invested well. Sabrina was going to have whatever she needed, he would see to it. If she wanted to shop like Whitney, then so be it.

Court had to restrain a grin at that last thought. Sabrina was too practical for that. Court was pretty sure he would have to do the buying if anything was bought for her.

"My God, they're from Senator Weston!" Whitney announced, her disbelief and confusion clear on her face. She laughed. "The old sly dog even apologized for everything that happened." She shook her head. "Can you believe that? After all the trouble he caused me, he thinks this will set things right?" She ripped the letter in half and tossed it onto the table.

"It's the thought that counts?" Kyle teased with his usual quick grin.

Whitney shot him a death-ray eye. "I have a few thoughts for him, none of which I can say out loud at the moment."

"How about us menfolk taking a walk down to the corral and checking out that stallion that's making us all proud," Austin suggested.

Frank quickly relinquished his tongs to his lovely wife. "Sounds good to me."

Court followed Austin, Kyle and Frank down to the corral. Charlie and Jewel were already there. Court didn't miss the little thing going on with their eyes. First Frank and C.J. Then Court and Sabrina, and Mrs. Cartwright and Mr. Ledbetter. Now Charlie and Jewel? There was definitely something in the air—or maybe the water—around here.

"I've already been offered five hundred dollars stud fee by a local rancher," Austin was saying, more than pleased.

"That's great." Court had heard of stallions that brought upward of one thousand dollars, but for just starting out, five hundred was an excellent fee.

C.J. shouted for Frank. Something about the grill. He excused himself and double-timed it back up to the house. Court was too busy studying the horse to pay much attention to what had been said. The animal seemed agitated.

Before Court could ask Charlie if anything involving the animal had happened before he and the men arrived, Kyle interrupted his thought.

"Daniel says you're planning to get the Korbett breeding operation up and running again."

Court pulled his attention from the horse. "Yeah, that's the plan."

"Court's got a lot more experience than the rest of us," Austin put in. "We'll need his expertise from time to time, as well. I hope you won't mind, Court."

One corner of Court's mouth hitched up. "Not at all. I'm looking forward to getting back into the business." Damn, he never thought he'd hear himself say that. But it was true.

Charlie and Jewel jumped down from the fence and trotted off. To have some privacy, Court supposed. The stallion bolted at the sudden move. He started a nervous trot around the corral.

"He's a damned fine animal," Austin said, pride in his voice.

Court instinctively backed up. "I think maybe there's—"

His ears laid back, the stallion reared and snorted. At precisely that instant Court saw the cause of the animal's distress. A snake lay basking in the sun at the edge of the corral on the far side. Before Court could shout any instructions the animal reared again, and then burst through the top rail of the corral. Austin threw his arms up to cut the animal off. The horse reared again, neighing his frustrations.

Court slowly moved closer to the animal. "Stay back, Kyle," he instructed when the other man took a step toward the horse. "Austin, move to your—"

Austin advanced on the horse and it reacted. As if in slow motion, Court shouted *"No,"* but it was too late. The horse bolted and reared too close to Austin, knocking him backward. Austin hit his head on the side of the barn as he stumbled back, then crumpled to the ground and lay motionless.

"Don't move," Court ordered Kyle again. He knew the man wanted to help his friend, but one wrong move could send the horse into another frenzy. Those powerful hooves were way too close to the downed man. Way too close.

Years of instinct and refined skill took over as Court

eased closer to the nervous animal. He murmured the sounds his father had taught him that would soothe. He eased a step closer, then paused, careful to maintain eye contact with the horse at all times. Another step, another hesitation, until the animal's eyes told him it was okay to move again. Court could see the horse struggling with his own curiosity. Just a couple more steps, a few more softly spoken words—

Austin stirred, groaning loudly.

"Don't move, Austin," Court said in as low and gentle a voice as he could marshal at the moment. "Just don't move."

The disturbance cost Court a tiny degree of trust, he noted instantly. The stallion backed up a step, his right rear hoof now dangerously close to Austin.

Kyle kept the others at bay with an uplifted hand.

"Come on, boy," Court murmured softly. He gained another foot or so, recovering that one step back he'd taken in the animal's perspective. At least two full minutes later, sweat trickling into his eyes, Court got within arm's reach of the horse. Seconds turned to another minute before Court slowly stretched out his hand for the horse to inspect. Hesitantly at first, the stallion nudged Court's hand, then smoothed his muzzle over his palm, surrendering. Court restrained the sigh of relief he wanted to exhale. Not yet.

Turning slowly, Court faced the corral and slowly, ever so slowly, started to walk in that direction, coaxing the animal with gentle strokes to follow. Once inside the corral, Court looked around quickly for the snake. The ruckus had evidently sent the pesky reptile on its way.

Court patted the horse once more before slipping out of the corral to help Frank repair the top rail. Kyle had Austin back on his feet.

"You okay?" Court asked when Austin came up beside him.

"Yeah, fine. The knock on the noggin just stunned me a little." He rubbed at his head. "What the hell made that fool horse whack out like that?"

Court inclined his head toward the far side of the corral. "A snake. But it's gone now."

"Are you okay?" Whitney asked. She was followed by the other women who crowded around Austin, Molly trailing behind.

"I'm okay," he insisted, looking a bit sheepish. "Court here saved my neck." He grabbed Court's hand and pumped it once. "Thanks, buddy."

Court grinned and gave Austin's hand a squeeze before releasing it. "Oh, I can't say for sure that we saved your neck, but we—" he nodded toward Kyle, including him in the *we* "—probably saved you a trip to the emergency room."

Kyle scooped up his little girl. "*We* didn't do anything. You're the hero here, Brody."

Frank whopped Court on the back. "I say we have some grub on that one."

Court lagged behind as the rest moved back toward the house, still recounting the harrowing moments. Sabrina, Ryan in her arms, waited for him. When Court reached her, he slid his arm around her waist and pulled her close.

"You are a hero, you know," she insisted, her face aglow with pride.

He kissed the tip of her nose. "So are you."

She blushed. "I'm no hero," she denied. "I'm afraid of my shadow when it gets dark."

Court shook his head. "I know what you risked for Charlie and what you went through alone with the birth of our son. You have more courage than any woman I've ever known."

"Is that why you're marrying me, Brody, because you think I'm brave?" she teased.

"Mostly." Court grinned wickedly. "But partly because—" He leaned down and whispered the rest of his explanation in her ear, ending with the plans he had for her tonight.

Sabrina kissed his lips when he drew back. "You just remember all that because I'm definitely going to hold you to each and every promise."

Court took his son and followed Sabrina back to the house. Everyone was already lining up to fill their plates with the array of goodies arranged on the garden table. Whitney's unexpected bouquet served as a centerpiece.

The telephone rang somewhere inside the house, the sound reaching out to them through the screen door.

"Can't have a minute's peace," Mrs. McMurty grumbled as she broke out of the line.

"No, wait, I'll get it." Whitney dashed up onto the porch and hurried inside.

Sabrina suddenly turned and looked into Court's eyes, hers too somber. "Do you think that Ryan will remember the time we were apart?" she asked quietly. The worry etched on her face told Court the thought had only just occurred to her.

He shook his head. "Probably not." He smoothed the tips of his fingers over her soft cheek. "Besides, I'm planning on making up for lost time. I promise neither of you will ever be without me again except when I'm on assignment, and then only for a few days at most."

The worry vanished with the smile that widened across her lips. "Just another promise I plan on holding you to."

Charlie and Jewel skidded to a stop right beside them, interrupting the kiss Court had planned to bestow upon the woman he loved.

"Whoa, buddy, what's the hurry?" he asked a breathless Charlie.

"We were afraid we'd missed the food."

Jewel nodded her wide-eyed agreement.

Court started to ask where they'd been, but Whitney's shout stopped him. He pivoted toward the house.

"Daniel!" She bounded down the steps. "You've got to hurry!"

Austin and Kyle met her at the bottom. "What's wrong?" Austin demanded.

"Oh, God. I can't believe it!"

"Whitney!" Kyle grabbed her by the shoulders and gave her a little shake. "Slow down, tell us what happened."

Court passed Ryan to Sabrina and followed Frank over to join them. Whitney was scared to death; fear glittered in her round eyes.

"The phone," she croaked, then swallowed in an attempt to compose herself. "It was the department. It's bad."

Why would a call from the Department of Public Safety

put Whitney in such a tizzy? Montana Confidential was a branch of that department. They likely called regularly.

"It's a bomb," she blurted.

Court tensed. His gaze shifted immediately to Foster. Kyle Foster turned a deathly shade of white.

"They've found a bomb at the capitol building in Helena. They want all of you there ASAP!"

Court's blood ran cold. Could Neely have had an alternate plan?

No matter what happens here today, this destiny is already set.

* * * * *

Fall in Love with...

MEN
in UNIFORM

MUBPA10

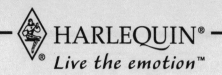

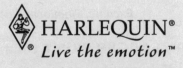

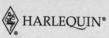

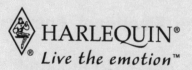

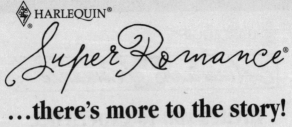

HARLEQUIN®

Super Romance®

...there's more to the story!

Superromance.
A *big* satisfying read about unforgettable characters. Each month we offer *six* very different stories that range from family drama to adventure and mystery, from highly emotional stories to romantic comedies—and much more! Stories about people you'll believe in and care about. Stories too compelling to put down....

Our authors are among today's *best* romance writers. You'll find familiar names and talented newcomers. Many of them are award winners—and you'll see why!

If you want the biggest and best in romance fiction, you'll get it from Superromance!

Exciting, Emotional, Unexpected...

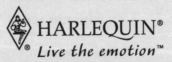

HARLEQUIN®
Live the emotion™